Who Is La Cucaracha?

"Who do you work for?"

A silence spread over everyone. Except for the raucous braying of some mules, the valley was shrouded in quiet.

The man barely managed to say, "La Cucaracha."

Slocum pointed at him. "Who is he? Tell us who he is?"

The man shook his head and shouted out loud, "I don't know. I never met him. Only the big bosses see him."

Don Carlos, lying on a blanket, nodded at the stone-faced Slocum standing above him. "See, I told you so."

No one had seen him—yet he led many gangs.

Unbelievable.

JAKE LOGAN

SLOCUM
AND THE
BANDIT CUCARACHA

JOVE BOOKS, NEW YORK

THE BERKLEY PUBLISHING GROUP
Published by the Penguin Group
Penguin Group (USA) Inc.
375 Hudson Street, New York, New York 10014, USA
Penguin Group (Canada), 90 Eglinton Avenue East, Suite 700, Toronto, Ontario M4P 2Y3, Canada
(a division of Pearson Penguin Canada Inc.)
Penguin Books Ltd., 80 Strand, London WC2R 0RL, England
Penguin Group Ireland, 25 St. Stephen's Green, Dublin 2, Ireland (a division of Penguin Books Ltd.)
Penguin Group (Australia), 250 Camberwell Road, Camberwell, Victoria 3124, Australia
(a division of Pearson Australia Group Pty. Ltd.)
Penguin Books India Pvt. Ltd., 11 Community Centre, Panchsheel Park, New Delhi—110 017, India
Penguin Group (NZ), 67 Apollo Drive, Rosedale, North Shore 0632, New Zealand
(a division of Pearson New Zealand Ltd.)
Penguin Books (South Africa) (Pty.) Ltd., 24 Sturdee Avenue, Rosebank, Johannesburg 2196,
South Africa

Penguin Books Ltd., Registered Offices: 80 Strand, London WC2R 0RL, England

This is a work of fiction. Names, characters, places, and incidents either are the product of the author's imagination or are used fictitiously, and any resemblance to actual persons, living or dead, business establishments, events, or locales is entirely coincidental.

SLOCUM AND THE BANDIT CUCARACHA

A Jove Book / published by arrangement with the author

PRINTING HISTORY
Jove edition / June 2011

Copyright © 2011 by Penguin Group (USA) Inc.
Cover illustration by Sergio Giovine.

ISBN: 978-0-515-14954-8

JOVE®
Jove Books are published by The Berkley Publishing Group,
a division of Penguin Group (USA) Inc.
375 Hudson Street, New York, New York 10014.
JOVE® is a registered trademark of Penguin Group (USA) Inc.
The "J" design is a trademark of Penguin Group (USA) Inc.

PRINTED IN THE UNITED STATES OF AMERICA

10 9 8 7 6 5 4 3 2 1

Prologue

Many simpleminded people worked for him on his hacienda. That was the reason he was overseeing the work being done in the corral with his livestock crew. He wanted to be sure they made no mistakes neutering the yearling colts. Mitch McCarty tossed back the lock of reddish hair in his face, reset his sombrero, then gripped the ropes along with the others standing behind a large yearling colt. They would soon gently lay the colt down on his side with the running W, a series of ropes tied to the colt's legs that two men standing behind the colt would use to gently pull the legs out from underneath him. Then Lano, the expert animal doctor, could operate on him. Mitch saw the fear in the yearling's eyes, as though the horse knew that they were about to take his future stallionhood away from him.

Two men eased back on the running W ropes, and the blood bay began to crumple despite his resistance. Lano and a stout boy were keeping him from falling down hard. The dust in the corral soon found Mitch's nose as he strained with the others.

"Easy. Easy now," he shouted. His horses were valuable products of his hacienda, and to lose one meant no *dinero* went into his coffers. To own and operate such a large holding, meet the payroll and the upkeep, was no cheap matter.

For him every horse, sheep, goat or cow and calf were important elements to his survival in this land of sharp cactus and rattlesnakes.

After the horse was eased onto the ground, he was quickly four-footed with large, soft, cotton ropes. Two ranch hands were on hand to be sure the horse did not strain or hurt himself. Their job was to distract him from fighting his binds.

"Good work. Good work," he told the crew. "Every yearling must be worked as easy as that. Do you see? No hurry. Work them easy."

Like children, the men began to bob their dust-coated sombreros in agreement, and white teeth flashed at him from many sun-dark faces. *"Sí, patrón."*

"Save my colts, mis amigos."

Lano pushed back the tall, dust-coated sombrero on his head as he knelt behind the horse's butt and looked at the exposed area. One man held the tail aside for him while a young boy scrubbed the area of the horse's genitals with soap and water on the bulge of the scrotum.

"Wash it good."

The youth told Lano he understood. Then another brought several knives and surgical tools on a Turkish towel for Lano's inspection. The veteran of a thousand such operations selected his surgical instrument and motioned for more men to sit on his patient so the horse would not strain.

His helpers in place, Lano made the first incision and the pink flesh peeled open, exposing the purple seed on the right side. He worked the walnut-sized nut and the trailing coiled cord out from the incision. Two men watched him closely as his understudies.

"Now, see how high he goes," Mitch said from over their shoulders. "If you do this wrong, you will have a proud cut horse who still thinks he's a stallion. That's no good. He will never have a colt either, but in his mind he thinks he can and will try."

"So you must cut off those ideas from the brain up there," Lano said, showing them the place on the cord. With a surgical clamp, he pinched down on the cord. The horse screamed for a short second, then his head collapsed on the dirt.

Next, Lano made a new slit and drew the other testicle out of the scrotum. Its connection too was pinched shut, and then both cords were sliced off behind the clamps. The double prizes were taken by a youth for the big fiesta planned for that night.

Another boy brought a pail of special paint and a brush to smear the contents over the entire surgical region. The wound dressing, which a *bruja* on the ranch had concocted for them, contained a repellant for flies and something to kill the germs.

Bearing the fresh, dark brown Flying M brand on his right shoulder, the gelding was released and soon stood hipshot, shaking off the dust in a cloud that engulfed everyone. He paused and then began to limp off as if in some discomfort, but after a few steps, he threw his head up and looked for his *compañeros*, giving a strong whinny. In a nearby pen they answered, and the gelding took leave of the corral in a run to join them. The workers cheered, closing the tall gate after him.

"Next."

Mitch told his *segundo*, Francisco, to watch that they did it right and started for the house.

Shouts and shots popping off made Mitch start and sent him up the corral rails to look for the source. From his perch, he could make out several armed men on horseback charging the hacienda with their guns blazing. He reached for his Colt revolver on his hip, but knew he could not do much with five shots to stop them.

"Bandidos! Bandidos!" he shouted and scrambled over the fence. His goal was to reach the big house. His wife, Martina, and his son, Reginald, were there. Son of a bitch, there must be a hundred raiders. Who were they? With giant steps, Mitch churned dust with his boots. Then at the sight of an attacker, he drew his Colt and fired into the face of the rider trying to cut him off.

The bandit flew off his mount. As the horse went by him, Mitch took hold of the horn, vaulted into the saddle and drew up the reins to turn for the casa. With four shots left in his

pistol, he found his way fraught with parked wagons and circled on the crazed horse. Then at his urging the mount flew
over a wagon tongue. Mitch kept his seat and raced for the
porch. Men were running all about. Women were bringing
them guns and ammo. His army was trying to assemble, but
the enemy was stinging them like mad hornets.

Whoever was doing this would pay with his life, Mitch
swore on his mother's grave. His horse tripped and went nose
down. He flew off over the horse's ears and rolled. Halfway
to his feet, something struck his left arm, and the pain shot to
his brain. Then another bullet found him in the shoulder. He
went facedown and blacked out.

Waking up with his face in the dust, Mitch could smell
smoke. A fiery pain ran up his left arm, which he discovered
was not usable. His mouth was full of sand, but he could not
spit, and the grit clung to his teeth. Wiggling his toes in his
socks, he realized the bastards had even stolen his expensive
handmade boots, leaving him for dead.

"Don't move, *patrón*. The men are coming for you," Francisco said, and Mitch tried to turn to see the man squatting
beside him.

"They shot me. What else did those bastards do?"

"Some of the men are putting out a fire in the casa."

"Martina? The boy?" He felt helpless lying on his belly.

"They took her. The boy is fine, the women hid him somehow."

"Damnit to hell, who was it?"

"They call him La Cucaracha, the Cockroach."

"Where does he come from?"

"I am not sure, *patrón*."

"Get some boys on horses. Give them some money. Tell
them to go find my amigo Slocum and tell him I need him to
go find my wife."

"Where will they find Slocum, *patrón*?"

"San Antonio. Or the coast. Sometimes he stays up on the
Sabine. Send several of them in all directions and tell them to
be quick—we need him now."

1

Small birds flittered in the mesquite tree limbs above Slocum's table on the patio. Consuela, a shapely young woman in a low-cut red dress, shook her hips as she danced and clacked castanets for him. Two Mexicans played soft guitar music to accompany her graceful shuffling and twirling. He raised his glass to salute her dance steps and shouted, "Olé," to send her spinning away like a double eagle coin on a polished bar.

When she finished entertaining him, she made a deep bow. He set down his glass and congratulated her in Spanish. "Ah, Consuela, you are such a dream of a woman. Come join me for a drink. Paco, bring those musicians a glass of cerveza, and bring Consuela one too."

Slocum reached over and patted her smooth brown forearm when she took a chair across the scarred table from him. "You are most generous to spend your afternoons with me, my love."

Regaining her breath, she beamed at his attention and words. "I love to dance for you."

"I realize that. You are so beautiful when you dance, I can feel it." He grasped the warm air in his fist as if he had captured some of her dancing in his grip. "Magnificent."

Paco delivered a fresh beer to Slocum as well as to the others. The older musician took off his sombrero and asked to be excused. Slocum dismissed him with an affirmative nod.

"Certainly, señor," he said. "But you must hurry back. We love your music."

"Oh, I won't be gone for long. Let no one drink my cerveza." They all laughed, knowing his intention was to empty his bladder.

"We will guard it with our lives," Slocum promised. Then he laughed as the talented man hurried away into the cantina.

Slocum stretched his arms out and absorbed the warm afternoon sun, glancing across the street at the dusty ruins of the old mission—the Alamo. If there was any parcel of land he wished to own, it would be someplace in south central Texas in the wintertime.

"Such a beautiful day to spend in such talented company. You, Consuela, one of the finest ladies I know, and these two great musicians. This one's name is Sid—and the older man?"

"Notcho," Sid said.

Slocum nodded. How much of this good life could he stand? He inhaled the smells of the city. Even the town's air smelled fresh. Soon the many buds would bloom and the bees would return. Under the table he felt the soft sole of Consuela's slipper teasing his shin. He winked at her, then glanced at the sun time. "Don't worry, my darling, we will soon go take a siesta—or whatever."

A horse's hooves clapped hard on the stone street as the animal and a young rider came into sight from around the Congress Hotel and galloped into the square. A hatless boy reined up his lathered mount and bailed off him in front of Slocum's table.

"Señor Slocum! Señor McCarty asks you to come at once to his hacienda."

"What's wrong, little one?" Slocum asked him in Spanish, rising to his feet.

"*Bandidos* have kidnapped Señora McCarty."

"Do you know their names? These *bandidos*." Slocum

was shocked that anyone would bother anything that Mitch McCarty owned.

"Señor, they call him La Cucaracha."

Slocum considered the matter with his eyes closed. The Cockroach. The name meant nothing to him. But Mexican bandit leaders sprouted like mushrooms after a spring rain.

"What will you do?" Consuela asked, looking wide-eyed at him.

He collapsed in the chair and shook his head. His palms turned up in defeat. "I must get my horse now and go see my amigo McCarty in Mexico at once."

"But what about me?" She turned her lower lip out to show her disappointment.

"Cross your legs for a few days, my dear." He winked at her. "I won't be gone very long."

He tossed two silver dollars to Sid for him and the old man, then spilled a wad of folding money from his pocket on the table for Consuela. She shoved the bills down the front of her dress between her glorious cleavage and then she flew over to kiss him good-bye. . . .

Two days later, Slocum wondered if the whole episode in San Antonio had been a dream. In his mind he tried to revisit those moments in the Alamo Square, but the desert conditions around him blocked out the reality of the peaceful times he'd spent there. In his vision now, Consuela appeared fat, lethargic and lazy, with legs as thick as an elephant's and a huge butt that she rolled around rather than whirled, hardly able to move the great expanse of flab.

He tried to shake all the morbid images that lingered with him while he studied the heat-wave distorted desert that made the faraway hills appear fuzzy. Nothing in his mind made good sense with what he recalled. One thing he felt certain about: He had not taken a drink of anything but canteen water and a single shot or two of whiskey in two days of travel. He began to wonder if there was something else going on, if perhaps he was under a spell.

Late in the afternoon he rode up on a dusty cluster of jacals populated with bleating goats and shrill-sounding children. He stopped to see if he could find a *bruja* in the population. Only a witch could have cast such a spell on him, and that meant only another could remove it.

At the first jacal, he stopped and dismounted before the doorway. A woman in her twenties came to the door, holding back her small children with her hands.

"*Sí*, señor?"

His hat in hand, he nodded. "I am looking for a *bruja*."

"*Bastardo*," she spat at him. "You would come and ask for such a thing with my children here? Have you no manners? Have you no decency?" Then she closed the canvas curtain door. From behind it she shouted obscenities at him. "Get away from me. Are you mad?"

Slapped in the face by her raw anger, he stepped back a few steps and reset his hat. He felt weak-kneed, as if he had only half of his usual strength. Was he dying? How could he tell? He had no fever other than the warmth on his face from the sun's rays that bore down so relentlessly on him.

He searched around for a man to question, since the women in this place took such affront at his asking after a *bruja*. Several men turned their backs at his questions, and some threatened him for even asking about such a person.

A woman came to her doorway and beckoned him to come over. She had the image of a mature woman. Not the fairy-like thinness of a barefoot girl making ballerina strides over a field of wildflowers, but with the ripeness of an apple, polished and handsome. All of her firm movements under the dress's material invoked the power of seductiveness. With her sleepy, deep brown eyes, she looked like a woman freshly arisen from a bed of all-consuming sex.

"Can you help me? Someone has cast a spell on me." His knees threatened to sag when she stood on her toes and reached up to look underneath his eyelids. She raised each of them as if to search for something hidden behind them.

"Have you ever had a spell cast on you before?" she asked, with a voice that sounded like smoke.

"Not like this one."

His sleeve caught by her long hand, she guided him inside, out of a swirling dust devil. As the door closed, he felt as if he had escaped something that had been clutching him. "My horse—"

"He is in no danger. I can care for him later."

"Am I under a spell or a curse?"

She looked him up and down, then nodded slowly. "Someone, I fear, has been poisoning you."

"I wondered about that. Am I coming into its forces or am I going away from it?"

"I would say that you have been in the grasp of the power for some time, and only away from the source have you felt the bad effects it holds on you." She showed him the blankets on the floor to sit upon, then she took her place before him. She wasn't a teenager, but her smooth face and pert lips told him she wasn't used up either. "How long have you been away from that source?"

"Two days, I guess, if Consuela was the one putting the spell on me."

"What have you drank since then?"

"Canteen water and some whiskey. I had a pint in my saddlebags."

"We must dump them. They are most likely laced with her poison."

He agreed, for the first time thinking of those items as a source of his problem. "She might have planted some in it. I never saw her do it."

His gaze met her brown eyes. The woman sat cross-legged face-to-face with him and acted as if she felt deeply concerned about him and his plight.

"What will cure me?"

"Ah, some rest first. Then we will see if you are strong enough that you can will her powers away."

He took off his hat and she accepted it. Then she balanced on her knees in front of him, and when she took away his kerchief, her proud breasts under the dress brushed against him. She pushed his vest off his shoulders, then helped him stand. He toed off his boots and shed his pants. With his clothing on her arm, she rose and hung them neatly on wall pegs, his run-over boots in a neat row underneath them.

"Now lie back down."

He obeyed her and looked up at her ceiling, the exposed timbers as well as the brush and wattle of the roof. She returned with a brass jar and told him to roll over onto his stomach. Then with her powerful hands and the cool, oily liquid, she began to knead his tight back muscles. Within seconds, he became so relaxed he feared he must be falling through space. As though a rug had been pulled out from under him, he was in free fall, hurtling from space toward a faraway, hazy earth, and in moments was sound asleep.

When he awoke he discovered several soft candles set in a ring around him. Was he in San Antonio? No, he could hear the wind gnawing at the corners of the jacal. He was somewhere two days' ride southwest of there.

"Ah, the big man is awake," the woman said and took a seat on the pallet in a flutter of the ruffled hem of her skirt. Her bare legs flashed exposed as she sat upon them.

Slocum rose up on his elbows and nodded. "How long did I sleep?"

"A day and night."

"My horse?"

She gave a head toss toward his saddle, pads and bridle stacked by his clothes. "I said I would care for him."

He settled back and grinned at her. "The only thing you can't do is empty my bladder."

"Ah, you can go to the back door and go outside in the alcove."

He nodded, rose somewhat stiffly and went to the back door. Grit stung him and the wind howled passing by. But the main force of the whooshing air couldn't reach him behind the shelter of the adobe wall stacked high with dry desert firewood under a palm-frond roof.

When he returned she made him lean forward and put a thin poncho over his head that reached his knees, and she tied the sides. Then she stepped back to look at him. "You are covered."

"Was that important? That I am dressed. You showed little interest in my manhood when I got here."

She wrinkled her nose at him. "I am still a woman."

"Tempted?"

"Mother of God, when you got undressed, I saw immediately why that woman wanted you." She shook her head in disbelief that he didn't already know that for a fact.

He laughed and sat down again on the blanket pallet.

"Are you feeling better today?"

"Much better." He no longer saw elephant-sized legs on dancers or the antics of such fat monsters acting seductively toward him. Was what he'd seen only his imagination, or was she really an elephant-like creature who had cast a spell, making him believe she was Cleopatra?

"Do your ears still ring with small bells?"

"I hear the wind." He couldn't recall hearing any small bells, only church ones.

"No. Most men under such spells say they heard small silver bells the whole time."

"Thank God I didn't have them too. I was crazy enough as it was."

"You are a strong man or you would never have escaped her powers."

"Will they come back?"

"Sometimes—sometimes when you are worn out and tired they will try to come back to take you over again. When you don't have the will to fight them."

Slocum winced at her words. When he needed his senses the most, they could fail him. A man who lived on the edge of the law needed all of his powers in the toughest situations.

That was when he must have them, and not the depleting lost feelings of the days before. Despite the heat in the room, he shuddered and goose bumps pricked the backs of his arms.

"Is that from the residues left behind in me?" he asked.

She nodded. "You know what I mean? If you get drunk, the next day you drink some water and it occurs all over again."

He recalled that happening.

"Much the same. But if most of it is gone, your body can win a war against it when you're strong."

"Do you have medicine I could take to ward it off?"

"If I knew what she had used." She shrugged. "But I might give you the wrong thing and make it worse. You are doing fine for now."

"But an amigo of mine needs my help. A bandit has taken his wife and I need to help find her."

"It will be dangerous for you, being so freshly away from her. Her strength will wrestle with yours—she could defeat you like she did two days ago. You were very close to being eaten up."

Slocum made a pained face at her. "How would I have acted?"

"You have seen men seated on the ground in Mexico holding out a tin cup and unable to walk?"

"*Sí.*" He'd seen them all over that country, even in places like San Antonio. "But I thought they were faking. Too lazy to work."

"No, señor, they have been possessed by some vicious *brujas*, and since they could not have them, they in turn destroyed these men mentally and physically."

Slocum narrowed his eyes at her. "But I told her I'd be back."

"Obviously"—she hunched her left shoulder and made a face—"she does not believe you and has shed her wrath on you for leaving her."

He dropped his chin and considered his condition. What this woman had just said did not inspire much confidence in him.

"I have some *cabrito* and beans ready for you. You must be hungry."

"I can eat anytime."

"Good, then drink some wine. Red wine will calm and clear your thoughts." She poured him some in a goblet and handed it to him. The rich grape product did ease his tongue and went down well.

She moved closer and scrubbed the stubble on his cheek with her palm. "Maybe if I shave you, it will cheer you up."

"Oh, I'm cheerful enough, and I'm grateful. Why do these people of the village hate you so?"

"I am unsure, except they know I am a *bruja* and as such I could cause trouble."

"You have a man?"

"I have you."

He nodded that he'd heard her and finished his wine. She poured him more and for the first time used her brown eyes to flirt with him. It made him feel much better. He couldn't have raised a hard-on only two days ago. At the moment his shaft felt ready to spring to life if she acted the least bit excited about doing it. Feeling back to normal was reassuring enough.

The goblet raised, he toasted her. "Here is to the greatest doctor I have ever known. *Gracias*."

"They call me Angela."

"Slocum."

"Nice to meet you too, big man." Angela laughed and raised her eyebrows. "Now I am the one who is on the defensive. I can see why she wanted you so confused that you would go back to her."

"Hell, I can't do that to McCarty. I should be down there right now helping him."

She shook her head. "For the moment that man is no concern of mine. Do you remember me rubbing you down? I know you are a man of steel. Your body is bound in corded muscles. I bet you made her faint many times when you had sex with her."

"Most of the time."

She nodded and smiled confidently at him. "Should I shoot off the starting gun for us?"

"No hurry."

"What would you like me to do first?" Her hand on his shoulder, she rose to stand on her bare feet.

"Dance for me," he said.

The reflective light from the fireplace drew shadows of her on the plastered wall. She raised her arms snakelike toward the ceiling until they were circling as high as she could reach on her tiptoes, then she clapped them together. Whirling round and round she dipped lower and lower. She was turning at such a high rate of speed, he had no idea how she could do it.

Unable to resist the temptation, he caught her in his arms and pulled her down onto the blanket beside him. His mouth closed on hers, and he felt the ripple of pleasure move over her. His hand felt her breast through the material of her blouse. He'd never in his life been in such a blur that he could recall.

In instant response, her tongue touched his lips, then probed his mouth. Sex with Consuela had been good, but Slocum realized that getting involved with a woman as mysterious as Angela was an entirely different situation. Their mouths told of their needs with wet kisses.

Still short of breath, Angela uttered a moan when his hand slid over the slight swell of her belly and under her waistband, then serpentlike sought the V between her legs. Belly to belly, they sought a needed closeness to be one.

With her blouse pushed aside, he kissed her pointed naillike nipples as if tending them, and then his lips covered her mouth. By then she was trembling all over, and when free of his kisses, she gulped for more air. After exploring her all over with his hands like he couldn't get enough of her smooth skin, he rose above her.

She pulled him down on top, spread her legs apart and gathered her skirt, and when his erection entered her, she clutched his upper arms. He stroked forward, falling into the rocking rhythm as old as time of man and woman giving pleasure to each other.

In the growing fervor, she raised her butt off the blanket to meet his charge, and the muscles inside her began to close on him. Their wild friction heightened their excitement until his volcano erupted, and he felt her clutch him as their world flooded and they collapsed on the blanket.

"Oh." Angela sighed and swept the dark brown hair from her face. "No wonder she tried to keep you under a spell."

Braced over her, Slocum smiled, and for the first time in days, he felt like himself again.

She raised herself up on the pallet and listened.

"Horses," she said and looked perplexed as she and Slocum separated and rose to their feet.

His fist was filled with his .44, which he'd grabbed from the nearby holster, but she put her hand out to stop him. "I'll go see who they are."

He set down the gun and quickly pulled on his pants.

She straightened her clothing on the way to the front door.

"Who's there?" he asked.

With a shake of her head, she looked out from the partially opened door.

2

She eased the door shut behind her. "They are only vaqueros. They come to visit some *putas* in this village."

"No problem?"

"They won't bother us. I am sorry they interrupted us." She helped smooth the shirt he'd buttoned, then she traced her fingertips over his chest.

He swept her tight against him and kissed her. "Not your fault."

"Where will you go now?" She tossed her slightly waved hair back over her shoulder.

"To see my amigo and help him."

"May I go along with you?"

He thought about it for a split second. "It may be danger-ous for you."

She smiled. "I am not afraid."

"Where can we get you a horse?"

"My neighbor has one. She would sell it cheap. Five to seven pesos?"

"Is it any good?"

"Good enough to ride out of here on."

"I have some money." He dug in his pants pocket for it.

"Let me go buy it. She will ask too much for it from you."

He agreed and counted out ten dollars. "I can wait here," he said. "But not too long."

With a wink, she shared a grin with him, then hurried off to secure the horse—he sat on the pallet and drank more wine. The wind was still blowing strongly outside. She soon returned through the back door.

He scrambled up and went to see her purchase. There was another woman who'd come back with her standing in the porch area. Dressed in a wash-worn dress, a rawboned woman with a square jaw and none of Angela's beauty held the reins while Angela put woven pads and a Mexican saddle on the gray horse.

"Valrey, meet Slocum," Angela said and quickly cinched the girth on her horse.

"Here, can I help?" Slocum asked, nodding to the woman.

"No, I have it done. I must go get your horse now."

Before he could protest, Angela hurried off. Slocum and Valrey were left alone with only the wind still protesting at the corner of the shedlike porch.

"She is a good woman. She says a *bruja* has you in her spell."

Slocum chuckled. "I guess she did have anyway."

"Angela is a good one to help people. She has helped me. My first man was killed in a train crash. She found me another: Martino."

"He is a good man?"

"Oh, yes, very." She blushed. "He wears me out when he comes home from his job deep in Mexico."

"Does he work down there?"

"*Sí*, in the San Phillipe Mines. He sends me money and takes good care of my other children from my first marriage."

"Does he come home often?"

"No, no, it is a long ways down there and back. But he comes home often enough that I am always pregnant." She cradled the bulge of her low belly in both hands and grinned at him.

"You must be blessed then," he said to make small talk.

Angela returned with his horse and he tossed on the pads and saddle. Then he began to buckle it down.

"I will get some bedding and food," Angela said.

He agreed and dropped down the stirrup. Valrey came over and spoke to him, looking off at the gust-swept, dusty desert. "If she is ever not here next time, come to my casa. I am not as pretty as her but—you know what I mean?"

He nodded. "That is very kind of you to offer."

She shrugged. "Someday you may see your way back here, huh, hombre?"

Then Angela was ready. She tossed the blanket roll for him to tie on behind his cantle and hung two sacks of things over her horse and then bound them on.

In a flash, she hugged her friend and kissed her cheek, then she ran to her horse, ready to ride out.

"Good-bye," Slocum said to Valrey and pulled down the brim of his hat. Then he swung Jocko, his big bay horse, around.

They set out in the dust storm toward the southwest. His biggest dread was that the storm might increase, shut off all their vision and cut off their chance to get to his friend's place.

With his head bent into the gritty blasts and hers under a scarf, they moved through the sharp wind that cut a swath out of Mexico. They reached Villa Verde by sundown.

"Ah, mi amigo Slocum," the *patrón*, Don Juarta, said from the lighted front porch. "My men will take your horses. And to you good evening, señora." He bowed and swept his hat on the floor to her.

"Gracias," she said, looking all around as if to take everything in.

"Her name is Angela," Slocum said, giving his reins to the man waiting for them, who held his sombrero over his heart.

"Ah, such a lovely lady. Welcome to my hacienda, Angela. Tomorrow I will show you the entire ranchero."

"I am afraid that we must continue in the morning to

Mitch McCarty's. He sent for me. A boy said someone had kidnapped his wife."

"Oh, yes, I know. That is so terrible. Yesterday I sent four pistoleros over to help him find her."

"Good. What happened up there, and who did this?"

"I only heard short bits, but they were all bad. I have guards posted all around my holdings. McCarty lost his left arm and took some more bullets, they said. The leader was a bandit who calls himself La Cucaracha."

"Never heard of him before this." He looked at Angela.

She made a slight "no" sign to him and then smiled for their host. "Ah, such a great hall," she said after her first view of the two-story open room.

"I have many lovely things, my dear." He boasted with pride and told the woman standing in the doorway at the side that they had guests; she must bring them wine and food.

Slocum was amused at how Angela acted so impressed with the place. He handed his hat to a young maid who also took Angela's shawl and scarf.

Juarta showed them to the high-backed seats at the great table, Angela on the left and Slocum on the right of his head chair, which was larger and more kingly than the others. When they were seated, Juarta reached over and patted Angela's forearm. "You are lovely, my dear. It is so nice to have you here as my guest. Where do you live?"

"San Antonio," she lied, unfolding the linen napkin.

"Ah, where civilization abounds, no?"

She nodded.

"Someday you must invite me to your casa. I go to San Antonio quite often."

"My casa is being remodeled," she said. "Perhaps when the work is complete you might come by."

"When will it be done?"

"Next year, they promise, but you know lazy workers."

"Ah, I have many. Slocum, you are very lucky to have such a fine lady to accompany you down here."

"She was tired of the hammering," he said, hardly able to

contain his amusement at her fabrications. He toasted both of them with his wine goblet. "To good health."

"Such a shame this incident happened at the McCarty Hacienda," Juarta said. "I hope you can sort it out for him. First the Apaches, now *bandidos*. They need to send some soldiers up here."

"The Apache days aren't over either," Slocum said as the servants brought out enough food for an army.

"But most of them are over in Sonora. Not like the old days, when the Comanche came down here as well." Juarta shook his head.

Throughout the meal the conversation went on about taxes and the central government in the federal district and its lack of concern for everything but the gold and silver brought out of the *Norte*. Juarta made several passes at Angela, which amused Slocum. The poor man had no idea she was a *bruja*—perhaps she had sprinkled stardust around the room to attract him. Juarta was, for Slocum's part, close to embarrassingly struck by her beauty.

Slocum and Angela retired to their own room at last. Their host had offered them two bedrooms, but Angela had told him one was fine. The notion did not faze him, and a maid showed them to the larger quarters.

Slocum toed off his boots. "Tell me, do you have plans for Juarta?"

"Do I hear a jealous tone in your voice?"

"No, I simply wondered."

"This would be much nicer quarters than my casa, wouldn't you say?" She held out her hand to the rich items in the soft candlelight and the great feather bed in the center of it all.

"Nicer, not better."

"Ah, but I must think about such things. Someday I will be old and wrinkled. Only old winos and whoremongers will want me. Before my looks die"—she began unbuttoning his shirt—"I would like to live under such a roof."

"Ah, I agree that you should. I can leave you here if you wish."

"No, the time is not right. That is why I took your room—well, partially why. I didn't want to spoil Juarta's greed for me by letting him climb in bed with me tonight and having a wreck the first time." She hung her dress on the ladder-back chair and turned back to Slocum with the candlelight flickering over her ripe body.

He dropped his pants and stepped out of them. "What kind of a wreck?"

She winked at him. "Juarta would get so excited in bed that he'd spew his cum all over my belly before he even got inside me. Besides, I have you, and I know I will sleep tight when you finish with me."

He kissed her and drew her nakedness against his bare skin. There was no end to what a witch would do to get what she desired—he'd seen one in action that evening and understood her ways. This hacienda would be much better than her casa in a settlement that had no use for her. Hugging her to him, he felt his erection grow between them. Morning would come too damn early, and it sounded like his amigo McCarty was in tough shape. But that was tomorrow's worry. For tonight, Slocum put his concerns aside and lost himself in a wild lust for Angela's flesh.

3

On horseback they rode side by side and pushed hard from before dawn for the McCarty Hacienda. Their refreshed horses made good time. By late afternoon, Slocum noticed the tired edge that Angela tried to mask from him. Then as the sun fell into a bloody death beyond the Madre foothills, they reached the edge of McCarty's orchards.

"Have you ever been here before?" he asked her as they short loped through the orchards.

She shook her head.

"It is an impressive place. McCarty is an engineer and has set up an irrigation system for all these fruit trees, crops and grapes. It is very interesting."

"Is he a gringo?"

"An Irish prince, I believe, who was educated in Europe, roamed the seas and ended up here. You will like him."

She made a that-would-be-fine face and winked. "I will like being with you."

"Fine. I hope my friend is healing."

"I feel he will be, but after all he has suffered, he will still have a long way to go."

"If you believe he is healing, I feel better already."

"Halt, señor," a guard ordered, backed by two rifle-bearing men who stepped into the road beside him. "What is your business here?"

"My name is Slocum. Your *patrón* sent for me. This woman, Angela, is with me."

The man doffed his sombrero. "Señora and señor, welcome to the hacienda. My *patrón* anxiously awaits your arrival. Diego, get your horse and show our special guests to the casa."

"We can find our way," Slocum said.

"No, señor, we are all so upset about the kidnapping of Señora McCarty and the raid made upon us, in the twilight someone might mistake you for a bandit."

"I don't want to be killed," Slocum said and nodded for Diego, who was mounted on his horse, to go ahead.

At the house, the horse handlers came quickly and took their horses' reins. Diego, hat in hand, introduced the two of them to the straight-backed woman at the door.

"Señor Slocum, this is Leona," Diego said.

Slocum removed his hat and shook her hand. "Leona and I know each other. This is Angela."

"Ah, at last you come," the tall, proper woman said. "The *patrón* is sleeping. If you two wish to eat first, we will let him sleep awhile longer."

"That will be fine." Angela agreed.

Leona took Slocum's hat and Angela's shawl. "Come with me."

"We can eat in the kitchen," he said, shooing the woman on. "We aren't that fancy."

"The señora better never find out." Leona looked to the high ceiling for help from her saint.

Slocum laughed. "Señor McCarty's wife, Martina, is very proper," he said to Angela.

"And I wish she were here," Leona said. "We have not heard what ransom he even wants for her."

"The note will come." After this hombre La Cucaracha had all the pussy he wanted from her, he'd get serious about money. Slocum stepped into the kitchen, and everyone on the staff grew stiff backed and very somber.

"You all know Señor Slocum, and this is his lady—"

"Her name is Angela."

They all said hello, welcomed them, then went back to work, or at least made it look like they were working.

"They are very hungry. What do we have to feed them?" Leona inquired of the crew.

"Roast beef," one girl said.

"We can make fry bread," another volunteered.

"We have some enchiladas that are still warm."

"That's plenty. Sounds great to us." Slocum glanced aside, and Angela agreed.

"Sit at the table." Leona gestured to the table, and Slocum thanked her.

The meal went well. Angela gushed over their wine and exchanged some words about the meal with him. When they finished eating, their hostess led them through the great hall and to the door of a bedroom, rapping on the door. Mitch called for them to come in.

In the room's soft candlelight, Leona helped Mitch sit up in the bed, bracing him with many pillows. He was anxious for her to get through with her fussing but smiled at Slocum. The glaring thing for Slocum was that McCarty's left arm had been amputated at the shoulder and his chest was wrapped in bandages.

"Hell of a fine mess I'm in, ain't it?" Mitch said, looking disgusted. Clean shaven and with his red hair cropped shorter than Slocum had ever seen it, he looked pale under his red freckles.

"I understand they really swept in here on you?"

McCarty closed his green eyes and shook his head. "Like locusts. Most of us were working young horses at about eight o'clock in the morning, and they came in here like Apaches. Caught us off guard. I had no idea. Women rushed arms to the men. Three of them were murdered saving the hacienda. Several women were raped before my men took the hacienda back, and those bastards swept my lovely Martina away with them."

"Leona told us there was no word of ransom so far?" Slocum made the statement a question.

"So far they've cut my bloody arm off me and dug two bullets out of my back, but no word on Martina. I'd give my very life for her safe return."

Slocum took a ladder-back chair and pulled it up close to sit on. "Who can tell me all that I must know about this bandit?"

"The Cockroach, they call him. He must stay up in the Madres. Not many know much about him that I can find out. I have pistoleros all over listening and looking for him, and I get no word back."

"Juarta said he sent you four men."

"Yes, yes. Good men. I gave them money and sent them to go look for her as well."

"You think he's in the Madres?"

McCarty winced in pain from some small movement, then quickly said, "Aye, lad, I think the likes of them are up there."

"Is there an Apache among your workers or someone who speaks their language fluently?"

Slocum exchanged a nod with Angela. He wanted someone adept at talking to the Apaches. They knew what went on up there.

"Cherrycow," Leona said to McCarty as she fixed the sheet over his lap.

"Oh, yes, there is a man who lived with them for several years, as good as was an Apache. Leona, send for him. Also, have someone bring us back some Irish whiskey and some glasses. I'm tired of this raw mescal." Leona nodded to a girl by the door, who slipped out to perform the errands. Then, as if he had not noticed her before, McCarty waved Angela into the light beside the bed. "I am a man of such poor manners, and he wasn't going to introduce you to me."

"Her name is Angela," Slocum said.

Angela smiled at McCarty. "And you were so busy with the business of your wife. I do not feel slighted."

"Bah on business. I am so tired of this bed I could burn it. Aye, but I am concerned for my lovely wife and her treatment at the hands of those worthless heathens."

"Rest," Leona said, holding his hand and then slowly releasing it. "You have much longer to go to be able to take any trail."

"But I am so tired of this bed—"

She shook her head. "Your anger won't rush your recovery."

He agreed with a solemn nod and looked back at Slocum. "What are your plans for this Apache?"

"If he knows the language, we can talk to them," Slocum said. "They will know where this man hides in the mother mountains. A rock is not turned up there that the Apaches do not know about."

"I never thought about them."

"They may help us find the Cockroach, for a price."

"How much would that be?"

"I don't know, but I'll let you know."

"I have money. But I would have to get large sums from faraway banks."

"Wait till you hear from the bandits or from me."

Mitch narrowed his eyes. "I need her back."

"I understand, but you know how vast a country it is to search for her in."

"Yes, I've been over lots of it. How many pistoleros will you need to take with you?"

"Besides the Apache man, perhaps two more tough hombres. I don't want a super large party. Too many men and you can't move fast enough when you need to."

"What else?"

"I can arrange all the rest with your people. You should rest," Slocum said, concerned they were wearing him out.

"Damn, I'm sorry to interrupt your life—but I have to have my son's mother back."

"Angela and I had nothing else to do." Slocum laughed and shared a smile with her as the good whiskey arrived.

Later in their own room, Slocum and Angela undressed and talked about his friend and the tough situation he was in.

"What do you think?" Slocum asked her.

She shook her head. "He is a survivor, like I suspected. But he will be many weeks recovering, and he is like you. You'd be a poor patient."

Slocum hugged her neck and then bent over to kiss her. "I would be a good patient."

"Not with your arm missing. His loss makes him worry much about what he will do when things are like normal at his ranch. He worries they've stolen his virility."

She shed her dress over her head and stood as naked as Eve when she turned back to face him.

"He wasn't shot down that low."

"A man's mind has more to do with that than his missing arm or any other body part."

Looking at her ripe body took away Slocum's breath, so he hugged her to his own. "Like me. I have problems."

Pressing her exposed mound against his growing erection, she laughed aloud. "Sure you do, silly man."

They scrambled into bed, tickling each other and giggling like two children, Slocum finding spots she absolutely couldn't stand him touching without her laughing. Finally, with their fingers locked, he pressed her down on the bed and moved on top. Then using his hips, he swung his pendulum around and hunched the nose of his great stick into her gates.

She threw her head back, spread her thighs wider apart and moaned. "God, that feels so wonderful."

They untangled their hands and he reached under her, clutched the hard cheeks of her butt and drove his spear to the bottom of her depths.

"Yes! Oh, that feels awesome. . . ."

For him too.

Before sunup, one of Leona's helpers knocked on the door. Slocum woke with his face buried in a goose down pillow. In a dry voice, he managed, "We're coming."

"Sí." And the helper was gone from outside the door.

"Who's we?" Angela asked, moving away from his threatening hands. "Damnit, I can sleep in, can't I?"

Off the bed, he still came back after her. "No. No, we need to head for the Madres tomorrow morning, and we have much to plan for and get ready."

At last, with Angela up and Slocum pressing her against the door, he made a trap by planting his hands on the wall on either side of her shoulders and then kissed her. She savored his mouth hard. He soon reached between her legs and teased her clit with his middle finger.

"Oh, no." She moaned and moved her hips toward his rising appendage.

"Oh, yes."

When they finally walked across the great hall from the wings, Leona was standing in the kitchen doorway, arms folded.

"Francisco is here, and so is the Apache," she said. "You are late."

"Sorry, we must have fallen asleep again," he said and ushered Angela ahead. "You start eating. I'll speak to my guests."

A kitchen girl served him a mug of steaming coffee, and he went to talk to the tall man by the door.

"You must be Francisco." Slocum shook the man's hand. Tall for a Hispanic, Mitch's *segundo* looked at him eye to eye. They stood at the back door of the kitchen and then stepped outside to talk in private.

"I have the one who lived with the Apaches here. We call him Cherrycow."

"I will speak to him. You must have lots to do."

"That is no concern. Recovering the señora is the most important thing. Mitch said that you would probably like some mountain horses to ride up there?"

"Definitely."

"We will shoe a dozen for you today."

Slocum mentally counted four—no, five—riders and four packhorses. "Nine will be enough."

"There will be nine shod horses. He said you needed two pistoleros."

"Two is all, plus the Apache. Too many and you can't move fast enough when it is necessary."

"I agree. The toughest men I have are Obregón and Jesús. They will be ready to ride in the morning."

"Fine. What about supplies?"

"Leona is in charge of that. This is Cherrycow." Francisco waved a short man dressed as a peon over from a seat in the garden. "Cherrycow, this is Señor Slocum."

"Good to meet you, señor."

"Francisco, I imagine you are anxious to get things going. Cherrycow, come inside and eat with us."

"I can wait here till you are done, señor."

"My name is Slocum—no *patrón*, no señor. Come and meet Angela." He wasn't taking no for an answer and herded the shorter hombre inside the warm kitchen and out of the cool morning air outside the cookery.

Angela took Cherrycow's sombrero and ushered him to a seat. "Nice to meet you."

"*Gracias*, señora."

"Angela," she told him and offered him a selection from a large tray of food.

"Ah, so much to choose from. I don't know what to eat."

"Here," she said and began to fill his plate with fire-grilled meat, ripe fruit ready to eat, and pastries.

"That is plenty," he protested, trying to get her to stop.

She rose and put some food on Slocum's plate. "There, now you can talk between bites."

"You know the Apaches well?" Slocum asked the man.

"I was kidnapped as a young man and lived among them for years in the Madres. I even met Cochise when he was an old man. But one day, my wife and young son were picking berries with some others, and the Mexican army came and shot them. I was very sad, so I came back to my own people."

"The Apaches will know where we can find this Cock-roach. If we can find them."

"*Sí*, they will know. I know. I know how sad it is to lose a wife. I will try to find out from them where this bandit is hiding."

"Good. We'll ride in the morning for the Madres to find her."

"Will I need a gun?"

"You better have one. But don't worry, I'll have a gun and ammo for you in the morning."

"*Gracias* for the food. I will be here then, Slocum," the man said and quickly exited the kitchen, obviously too upset over something to stay there another minute.

Angela winked at him. "Too important a place for him to be in here."

Slocum agreed.

Leona rejoined them and looked after the departing Apache. "Cherrycow is a very loyal man."

"I imagine he is," Slocum said. "I've been thinking. Angela and I need to look less like gringos. Can you find us some mountain clothing?"

"Buckskin, huh? Big, well-used sombrero for you?"

"Fine."

"How big are you?" she asked Angela and had her stand. Then, as if satisfied with knowing her size, she told her *gracias* and to sit down. "I'll have the clothes laid out in your room tonight."

"Thanks," Slocum said and turned to Angela. "I'm going down to look over the horses Francisco selected. Not that I don't trust him—"

"Go," Angela said, shooing him away. "I better pack my few things today too."

He nodded and kissed her, then was on his way to the blacksmith shop. Gustoph, the man in charge, showed him the packsaddles and all the horse gear. The gear looked to be in good repair—Slocum also ordered some extra rope and girths for the journey. Gustoph agreed that he might need them.

The short-coupled bulldog horses, as they were called, were lined up in the alleyway being shod two at a time. The air was full of coal smoke from the forge used to heat and form the iron shoes. Mountain horses were small by most men's calculation, seldom over twelve or thirteen hands, but they were sure-footed and thick muscled. Real leaders, they could climb slopes larger horses would crumble off of. Slocum had great respect for them in the mountains.

"I gave you Baldy," Gustoph said. "He's bald-faced, but he is the toughest horse on the ranch."

"I'll take good care of him."

"I hope you can find the *patrón's* wife. She is a lovely woman. We all miss her."

"We'll try, mi amigo."

He made it back for lunch with Angela and met her in the great hall. "Leona wants you to try on the clothing she laid out for you in our room."

After their meal he went back to the bedroom and found the fringed buckskin pants. They fit. Next he tried on the pull-over shirt, and it fit as well.

Angela nodded in approval. "I think they belong to Mitch."

He took off the shirt and agreed. "I figure you're right." Then he removed the britches. "I'll save them for the ride."

She came across the room and hugged him. "Now we can take a siesta."

"Siesta, my ass." And he quickly kissed her. "You can stay here tomorrow if you like."

She poked him in his rock-hard stomach. "You aren't leaving me."

"Oh, all right."

She used both hands and shoved him backward in the bed and landed on top of him. "You are not getting away that easily."

His flesh warmed everywhere her fingertips stroked his chest.

Oh, hell, who needed a siesta anyway? Slocum thought.

4

Dawn found Slocum and his pack train and riders headed west of the last orchards on McCarty's land. Things were going well, and even his *bruja*, Angela, was surprised they'd managed to get it all together so easily. Slocum knew everyone on the hacienda wanted him off on a successful hunt for their lady—including himself.

The Madres were several days' ride to the west, though their sturdy mountain horses should make good time. Their group was well armed, carrying lots of supplies and a purse loaded with Mitch's money that he'd insisted Slocum take with him—Slocum expected to arrive at the base of the mountains with no problems in a few days.

"Where will we enter the Madres?" Angela asked, riding beside him as the day's heat and dust rose in their faces.

"Maybe Cuervo. There aren't a lot of people there to report that we are going into the interior, if this Cockroach has any informers."

"He probably does. Most of those kinds of men offer a generous reward for such information."

"I'll tell the men to spread the rumor we are simply going

to the Kinsey Mine to see an old friend. If they miss the McCarty brand on our horses, that might help mislead them."

"You have thought of everything." She shook her head as if amazed.

He reached over and clapped her leg. "No, not enough. I'm counting on you to help me."

"If I think of anything, I'll tell you."

He nodded, stood in the stirrups to look back and surveyed the line of his riders and pack animals. Deciding that everything looked good, he settled back down. "We'll water our stock at Coyote Wells tonight and ride on."

"We won't camp there?"

He shook his head. "Those desert outposts are usually controlled by trail pirates and are a good place to get killed in your sleep."

"I guess I had not thought about that."

"Have you stayed there before?"

"A man in my past and I stayed there one night."

Slocum nodded. "Maybe you were lucky."

"Maybe he was a pirate himself." Then she laughed. "I never heard them called trail pirates before. But the name suits many of them."

He agreed with a nod.

"I was young and didn't know about my powers back then. He was older and I thought he was so handsome. He wore a silver-mounted holster and acted so powerful with the black kid gloves he wore all the time."

"What became of him?"

"They hung him."

"Oh."

"The law in a small village arrested him for killing two unarmed men in a card game. There was a trial and the judge sentenced him to hang.

"I stole his horse from the livery and rode off the night before his execution. I cried all night long over losing him. Then when the sun came up, his face appeared before me in the sky and he told me not to cry anymore for him. That he was in peace and the money hidden in his saddlebags would take care of me."

Slocum nodded. "What did that teach you?"

"That I had powers and was a *bruja*. Others don't see and hear such things, only a *bruja* would. Like I knew when I first saw you talking to people and them scorning you that you needed me to help you."

"I was lucky then."

She shook her head and gave him a sly smile. "No, it was my good fortune you came along. That village was full of prejudiced people who hated me. I needed a new place and the real man who came along."

"How old were you when you rode off with him?"

"Not very old. He came to the village where I lived and I heard his silver spurs before I ever saw him ride into the square on a powerful black horse that day. I believed no great man like him would even look upon a skinny girl like me. But later he said he saw me that day and I cast a spell on him. He came back again three more times looking for me."

"How long before you saw him again and he took you away?"

"Two years, about. He rode in and I was busy washing clothes at the well. He stood by his black horse as the gelding drank deep from the trough. Impatiently he slapped the ends of his reins on his leg. When the horse was through, he walked over, still slapping his leather pants."

" 'What is your name, señorita?' he said.

" 'Angela,' I told him.

" 'You have a lover in this village?' he asked me.

"My eyes must have bugged out looking at him. What did he mean, lover? My tongue was glued down. I had no answer.

" 'I thought not,' he said. 'Come, I will buy you a new dress and we will be married.'

" 'What about this w-wash?' I stuttered.

" 'They will find it,' he said, dismissing it as nothing. Then he motioned for me to come to him, and he picked me up in his arms like I was a feather. He stepped up in the saddle and, still holding me, asked where my mother was at.

"I pointed over his head at the small church. 'With the Virgin Mary.'

"And he replied, 'Then no one here will cry for you.'

"He rode out of the village with me in his arms. Late that night he woke up a priest, who married us. After the short ceremony, he took me to a snug cabin in the mountains. We stayed a week up there on our honeymoon, then he took me to a woman who made three dresses for me. I thought he was rich. No one that I knew had ever owned three good dresses."

"What did he do next?" Slocum asked.

"I was so awed by him and his whirlwind ways with me in bed, I didn't know or care. I guess he gambled a lot and maybe even shot men for their money. Later I learned his name was not what he'd told me. But for almost a year, I was his simpleminded bride."

Slocum laughed. "Some story. What was his name?"

"The one I knew him by was Franco Cruces. But they said he was Juan López and he was wanted in Texas."

"So you were Mrs. Cruces?"

"I still am. I should wear black, huh?"

"How long have you been in mourning?"

She chewed on her lower lip as if she was counting before she spoke. "Maybe five years."

"Time to wear what you want to."

"Good," she said, and she sparkled in the blazing sun riding beside him.

They arrived in Coyote Wells at twilight. Slocum paid for the water for their animals and also to fill their canteens and two small barrels. The price came to three pesos. The man in the cantina-store stared hard at the silver coins Slocum put on the bar. Then, as if satisfied, the man nodded and picked them up with a muttered, *"Gracias."*

The riffraff standing at the bar looked him over and then turned back to a magpie-mouthed *puta* seated on the bar, who leaned back with her black hair–mounded crotch exposed and her short legs kicking back and forth to entertain them as she chattered nonstop.

One man, chewing on a stick, followed Slocum to the door. "You want some pussy?"

Slocum shook his head.

"No one's used her today. You could have her for a peso."

Slocum would rather use his hand to jack off than listen to her mouth the whole time they were in bed. "No, thanks."

"You may not find any for days going into those mountains."

"I'll take my chances." With that, he was outside under the palm-frond porch, hoping the pimp was gone.

"Anything there?" Angela asked when he rejoined them.

"A *puta* for a peso."

She laughed.

He nodded in approval at his men, who went about armed with rifles, just in case. Not showing them off or waving them around, but merely holding them in their hands, ready if they needed them, and they shoved them back inside their scabbards before mounting up. Slocum's train moved out, and he knew they had drawn more than one curious look from the loafers around the stopover.

Camped an hour later, the three men found dried sticks and dead mesquite branches for Angela to cook over. The coyotes started yapping at the dark. Jesús took a long gun and moved out of the firelight to keep an eye out for anyone or anything that could be a danger. The others sat in the firelight and laughed when Slocum told them about the magpie *puta* in the store-cantina. Angela fussed with the cooking, busily making flour tortillas with her hands, cooking them on a round metal sheet over the fire and boiling some beans.

Slocum took his lookout, Jesús, a cup of coffee laced with brown sugar. The man nodded politely and set his Winchester aside to take the cup in both hands.

"It is hot," Slocum warned him.

"Ah, but to have real coffee is a luxury for me." He blew

and then sipped on the tin cup, which he cradled in his kerchief to protect his hands. "And sugar is even better."

"A pistolero doesn't have coffee at his casa?"

"I have five children and a wife. Coffee is very costly."

Slocum nodded that he understood. "You must like this work."

"It is better than irrigating and hoeing crops. I have been a pistolero since I was sixteen."

"Were you born on that hacienda?"

"Oh, *sí*. I would live no other place."

"Have you been to the Madres before?"

"*Sí*. I met my wife up there and went back to get her."

"Does she have relatives up there?"

"*Sí*."

"Would they know about this Cockroach?"

"I don't know—but I will ask them if I see any of them."

"Angela will be ready to feed us soon. I'll whistle and you can come eat. I don't think the bandits up here are that industrious."

"What does that mean, in—?"

"It means too sorry to get off their asses."

Jesús laughed aloud. "*Sí*, I savvy that."

Another mournful coyote cut loose. "They sure are yapping a lot."

Jesús shrugged. "What is it anyway?"

"Just a coyote," Slocum said and went back to the fire.

After the meal, the three men told Slocum they would take turns keeping guard and promised to wake him before dawn. He thanked them, then took his and Angela's bedroll on his shoulder, and they went out in the desert to be alone. After he had kicked the sticks and rocks out of the way, he rolled the bed out. Then he toed off his boots and shucked off his pants.

She unfastened all the buttons of her dress. Then she took her sandals off. Her breasts gleamed in the moonlight, soft and tempting. She gave a little shimmy, and her dress fell to her ankles. Then she toed the garment to the edge of the bed-roll and stood naked before him. He let his gaze feast on those twin mounds of flesh that swayed gently as she took a deep breath. As he stared at her beauty, his rod straightened and she smiled. The nest of darkness nestled at the V of her thighs beckoned to him. He grew even harder. She hurried to get under the covers. He soon joined her, his rolled up gun and holster placed near his head.

They snuggled like lost lovers under the blankets, with him feeling her solid breasts and rubbing her flat belly, kissing her in open-mouthed fashion. Then their hands searched deeper until she helped him on top and he centered on entering her. They were subdued in their efforts and whispering about the finer things as he pumped his iron-hard erection into her, and their efforts heated up. At last deep inside came an eruption, and she raised her butt off the pallet to meet his charge. They collapsed in a heap to spend the night in each other's arms.

His last thought before he surrendered to sleep was, *What a* bruja *to have for my own. Thank you, Mrs. Cruces.*

5

The second day of the trip went uneventfully, and they camped that evening at a ranchero owned by a man Slocum knew, Hans Strycker. The tall German met him in the yard and nodded.

"I see you must be going gold hunting," he said, shaking Slocum's hand and looking over his pack train. He doffed his felt hat for Angela. "You are so unfortunate, child, to be going up there with this wild man."

"He's all right," she said and smiled at Hans, then bounced out of the saddle to shake his hand.

"Tell your men when they get the horses cared for to come to the back door. The help will feed them. You can come to the house. I am taking this lovely lady inside. Such bad manners you have."

"Her name is Angela. Mrs. Cruces to you."

Strycker waved him away and, with Angela on his arm, headed toward the lighted house. The two, busy talking, had no time for Slocum. He told his three men where to water and put up the horses, how to secure their food and where to sleep. They teased him and laughed about the man stealing his woman from him and how he better catch up with them.

"She'll be fine," he said with a laugh and started in the starlight for the main casa. Strycker had managed to ranch here, practically unharmed, for many years. Living in the path of the good and the bad that filtered in and out of the mountains was not easy. Perhaps he was tougher than Slocum thought, because the German knew how to survive and profit.

Angela brought Slocum a goblet of wine and led him into the dining room.

"Hans, tell me about this Cockroach," Slocum said, joining them.

"You don't know him?" Hans asked, crossing the room with a new bottle of wine.

"Never heard of him before this deal about him kidnapping Martina McCarty."

"Thinks he's some kinda damn generalissimo. He's been sending his men down here like he owns this trail. But so far he wants no war with me."

Slocum nodded. "Where is he staying?"

Hans shook his head. "I have no idea. I never go up into the mountains very far."

"Did you know that he had Martina with him when he came back?"

Hans shook his head. "No, but they had lost several men. I saw that many had been injured and shot up. They did not stay long here, only watered their animals and went on. Some were as much as two days behind the main party. They hauled many of the wounded ones back on travois."

"You never saw her riding with them?"

"No, but I did not bother with them. As I said, they watered their horses and then went on. I will call Estevan. He may be able to tell us."

"The food is ready, señor," a woman announced from the side door.

"Fine. Vinny, send word for Estevan to come up here."

"*Sí, patrón.*"

The kitchen help saw them seated, then began delivering

dishes. There was too much food for anyone to eat it all. But Slocum tried a little of everything.

"Estevan." Strycker wiped his mouth on a napkin and rose as the man entered the room. "Tell my amigo Slocum if you saw McCarty's wife with La Cucaracha."

"We heard they had kidnapped her, but no one who works here saw her go by with them."

Slocum wiped his hands on his napkin, then reached over to shake the man's callused, rough hand. "Did you think that was strange?"

"*Sí*, Señor Slocum. Very strange. This hombre who leads them is never with them. I have never seen him. If he kidnapped her, why wasn't she riding with his men anyway?"

"I have no idea. You see, she and McCarty are my very good friends. They shot him up in that raid. He lost his arm from one bullet and was shot two more times."

"I hope he is better."

"Yes, so do I. But I really need to find his wife."

Estevan turned his palms up. "If I could help you, I would. But these crazy people live deep in the mountains somewhere." He shrugged. "God be with you, hombre."

In the morning they rode into the foothills clustered with juniper and pancake cactus and more streams with water that came from the mountains. A village called Cuervo was Slocum's destination, and they arrived there in midafternoon. It was a sleepy little place in the deeper canyons with cottonwoods and some irrigated crops. Not a prosperous mining community, where gold or silver was mined, but a small agricultural settlement on one of the mountain entrance roads.

His men made camp outside of the scattered jacals. Since there was plenty of time left in the day, Slocum and Angela rode into town. He spoke to the padre at the mission church, a young man named Paul, who told him he knew little about this one they called La Cucaracha. Paul said that he'd buried two of the Cockroach's men who'd died on the trail when they came back from the raid on McCarty's hacienda, but he said he felt the names given to him were not true ones. He had not heard about the woman's kidnapping.

Slocum thanked him and handed him some coins for the poor box. Next Slocum started for a cantina and left Angela with the horses at the rack.

"I won't be long," Slocum said.

She nodded in agreement.

His eyes adjusted slowly to the dim light inside the smoky interior. Several men were playing cards at a table, and they eyed him suspiciously. The bartender came over with a bottle half full of brown liquid and a glass in his other hand.

"Drink?"

Slocum looked around and saw the card players had given up looking at him. He turned back and put a silver cartwheel on the scarred board top. The bartender glanced down at it, then met his gaze.

"La Cucaracha?" Slocum said under his breath.

The man shook his head.

Slocum noticed that the bartender seemed nervous and was looking often at the card players, as if he didn't want them to see him taking money. He put a ten peso gold coin on top of the silver coin.

The man shook his head. Then out loud he said, "I have no whiskey, señor. Only mescal."

Slocum nodded, started to pick up the coins and whispered, "If you hide the dragon he may come and eat you anyhow."

The bartender looked pale even in the low light and swallowed hard.

Slocum, with the coins back in his pocket, went outside and joined Angela.

"Learn anything?"

He shook his head and then swung into the saddle. "Fear has a grip around here on the little people."

"Powerful force," she agreed.

They rode back to camp and joined the others. Angela

headed for the fire pit while Slocum paused to speak with the men. "You have any relatives here?" he asked them as Obregón took both of their horses.

"No, señor. We will put the animals up. We have waited for the señora's good food. Jesús and I are good food burners." They all laughed.

"I may know someone here," Cherrycow said.

"Will you need some money to find him?" Slocum asked him.

The Apache, who had stayed quiet most of the trip but had been helpful to the others, smiled. "No, but I will go look for him."

Angela busied herself making a fire with the wood they had scrounged for her and getting food ready for her hungry crew. She sang a folk song about a wild horse that all the mountain people sang. Slocum felt grateful not to be in the saddle, and sat on the ground, hugging his knees. He was thinking about Angela's body and what he planned to do with it later.

Someone rode up and all hands went for their gun butts. The man nodded in the sundown's bright glare. "I am an amigo, señor."

"Fine. Get down," Slocum said. He noticed Jesús slip off to make sure this stranger had no one else coming behind him. In a few minutes, Jesús rejoined them.

"You are looking for the McCarty woman?" the stranger asked, removing his sombrero and bowing his head at Angela.

"What is your name? Do you know where she is?" Slocum asked.

The man looked around to be certain they were alone. "My name is Monte. I know her location, but I can only take one man up there."

"Monte, tell me where she is at."

"No, you would not pay me for the information."

"How much do you want?"

"Five hundred pesos."

Slocum shook his head. "That is too much for telling me something that may be a lie."

"I swear on my mother's grave I tell you the truth."

"Many men swear on their mother's grave. I don't know you and I don't trust you either."

"If I take you to her, will you pay me?"

"If she isn't there or if it's a trap, I'll kill you first." This hombre reminded Slocum of a cornered rat in a grain bin.

The man swallowed hard. "I savvy."

Slocum saw Angela cut him a cold look, then she turned back to her cooking. He could tell that she didn't trust this Monte and was upset that Slocum would even bargain with him. It'd be better to trust her judgment, but still, if Monte could get him into the camp—maybe he could buffalo his way out with Martina. He needed a lead on her location, and this might be the only one they would get.

He went for a cup of coffee and left Monte sitting by himself. When Slocum squatted down beside her fire, Angela snapped at him, "Who is that little rat?"

"Calls himself Monte. Says he knows where Martina McCarty is at."

Using a rag as a hot holder, he poured some coffee into his cup. When the pot was back in place, she checked on her beans with a wooden spoon. "I don't trust him."

"I know that."

"He is either not telling you the truth or not all of it."

"I'll be careful."

Her brown eyes pleaded with him. "Even careful can get you killed."

Slocum went back to the man and sat down. "Where do you live?"

"I have no home."

"How do you know where Señora McCarty is at?"

"I knew who the señora was, and when I learned where they held her, I knew that her husband would pay me for the information."

"Why stop to see me?"

The man smiled in the growing twilight. "Aren't you the man he hired to get her back?"

Slocum looked at the man and then he shook his head. Nothing in Mexico was a damn secret. Not a week on the road and the word had already reached the mountains ahead of his arrival that McCarty had sent Slocum to rescue his wife. At least, this bandit had been forewarned. He shook his head. "How far away is she?"

"Three days."

"I can cross these mountains in that amount of time."

"We have to go by the back ways."

Slocum wondered how much of what Monte said was true and how much was fabrication to extort money from him. Angela's opinion of this man should be a warning to him.

Jesús and Obregón soon finished with their horse chores and returned. Neither of those two acted very warmly toward Monte or were happy about his remaining in their camp. Angela soon made them tortillas to fill with her frijoles and fed her crew.

"Where is Cherrycow?" she asked, delivering Slocum some burritos.

"He is in the village looking for a friend."

She nodded that she had heard him. Slocum noted that she'd fed the man Monte and then sat by herself to eat. This must be a serious thing with her. Didn't she realize that sometimes he had to take chances to reach the means to an end? Maybe if he explained the situation better to her, she would understand.

By the time they finished supper, it was dark save for the stars. The moon would be late rising. The man Monte asked for permission to stay with them. Slocum agreed and shouldered his own bedroll. Angela nodded that she was coming, and when they'd gone a hundred yards away in the junipers, he cleared out the rocks and sticks with the sides of his boots.

She sat on the roll and shook her head. "I hope he does not cut your throat while we sleep."

He untied the roll and she rose for him to spread it. "Oh, I don't think he is a killer. He's one of those men who lives on the edge."

Even in the starlight he saw her scowl at his words. "He can't be trusted."

"I need to find Martina. Days go by fast."

"I don't want you dead. Who will find her when they kill you?"

"You, Obregón, Jesús and Cherrycow."

"Not me—"

He cut her off, catching her by the waist, then drew her close and kissed her. For a brief moment she fought him, but soon allowed him to kiss her and finally submitted to his attention.

"I don't want anything to happen to you," she whispered as he unbuttoned her dress to get to her bare flesh.

Then with a finger, he moved the hair aside from her ear and whispered, "I simply want you and your body."

She gave him a scowl, then began to help him undress. With his boots toed off, he dropped his gun belt to the bedroll, and she undid his pants, letting them drop to his knees. They soon were naked and secure under the covers.

His hand ran over her mound of stiff pubic hair while his hungry mouth fed on her breasts. She shook her head at him and finally got her warning out. "That man will either expose you to them or get you killed."

Then they were lost in their own physical pleasure and she spread open her love chest by widening and raising her legs for his entry. He soon was in place and she closed her eyes to enjoy his pounding. Damn, her womanhood felt like a vise clutching his throbbing dick. He savored the muscles in her body working with his for the most pleasure and they fell into a whirlpool that carried them away. This might be the last time for a while that they were able to share each other's bodies, and he intended to get as much of her as he could to remember her ways.

*   *   *

Before sunup the next day, Slocum met with Obregón, Jesús and Angela, and they made their plans. Cherrycow had not yet returned, so Monte was still their only lead on Martina's whereabouts. Slocum told the others wait for Cherrycow to come back, and then to go to a village, one he considered fairly safe, while he went with Monte to find Martina. The village, St. Francis, was a small community deep in the Madres. Several people would shelter and look out for them there. He gave Angela a list of the names of people to trust and some money for their needs. Then with only some supplies in his saddlebags, he kissed her good-bye

"I'll see you in a week or two in St. Francis."

She shook her head. "I know what he plans to do to you. I won't cry over your death. That man will kill you somehow, somewhere. I will not go to St. Francis. I will take my chances with that rancher Don Juarta. He needs me more than you do."

"I'm sorry you feel this way."

Damn, he hated to lose her. Perhaps he was being too headstrong about going with this man, but he felt that it was urgent to find Martina as quickly as possible.

"Here, take some money for the way to Juarta. You may need it."

She shook her head.

He reached down, forced her hand open, put thirty dollars in her palm, then closed her hand. "I'll have two of the men take you down there."

"I don't need anything from you." She shoved her clenched fists down at her side. "And I certainly don't need the men to show me the way to Juarta's."

With a nod, he stepped back. "I'm sorry, Angela. You were very generous with me. May God take care of you."

He stepped into the stirrup and hoped for another word with her. But when he swung his leg over the rump of his mountain horse, Baldy, he realized she had already left, and was gone from his life. But he waved to her back and rode off after Monte, who sat a thin bay mount. Slocum's belly churned over her bitter rebellion. Maybe he should have seen it coming. Booting Baldy in the sides, he made him trot to catch up with his man.

"Three days, huh?" Slocum asked him.

Monte managed to nod. Slocum dismissed him and rode on.

Only time would tell how this would work. He regretted most losing Angela and felt that he needed two sets of eyes to watch the "rat." But in his book, Martina McCarty was short on time to be rescued from those bastards. By this time, she had no doubt grown tired of all the pricks jammed into her since the attack on their hacienda. How had the Cockroach concealed her kidnapping so well? And did Monte know a damn thing about her location? If that rat planned to get any money for his spying, he better have knowledge of where they held her or, Slocum resolved, he'd feed him to the circling buzzards in the updraft overhead.

The buckskin clothing Slocum wore felt comfortable enough. It and the sombrero made him look more like the people who lived in the mountains. They passed woodcutters and pack trains moving rich ore from remote mines to the smelters on through the border. Monte ignored them. At least Slocum made note that none of them acted as though they recognized him. The climb into the pine country in the afternoon brought cooler temperatures. Monte told him they needed to travel north and Slocum agreed—it was his neck he risked.

They took a well-used trail headed in that direction. Slocum had never been on this path before, but many such ways existed crossing the range. Late in the day, his guide told him there was a safe place ahead for them to spend the night and get some food.

"Fine," Slocum said, looking around when he took a left at the Y in the trail.

"The village is down this way." Monte reined up his horse when Slocum didn't immediately follow him.

"All right." Slocum booted the bald-faced gelding after him. Something didn't add up. The man said they had to circle around to get to where Martina was being held. He understood that tactic, but until Monte told him more about this route, he wondered if it was all a hoax.

The village was made of mostly log cabins and some adobe ones. Maybe a dozen or so served as dwellings. Children busy at play stopped, grew silent and stared at the two strangers. Monte tried to make his pokey horse go faster, but it was no use. He rode up to a jacal, and a woman came out. Her arms folded, she looked critically at Slocum's guide.

"Nada, how are you?" Monte asked, dismounting. "Me and my amigo want to buy supper."

She held out her palm for payment. Slocum about laughed at the haughty look she gave Monte, as obviously she expected payment in advance. For sure, she didn't trust the peckerwood either.

"Pay her," he said to Slocum.

"How much?"

"Two pesos—"

"No." She stomped her sandal. "Three."

Monte shrugged. "I owed her more than I thought."

"Nada, is that all he owes you?" Slocum rode in close, smiled, dismounted and handed her the money.

The woman in her early twenties turned her attention to Slocum and made a pleasant face at him. She was short, as were most natives, and a little soggy around the waist, but she was prettier than most women in these remote villages. She obviously didn't trust Monte, and this new hombre she had before her had enough monetary attributes for her to show her graceful side.

She hooked her arm in his and invited him to come into her jacal. On the way, she dropped the coins in between her proud breasts. At the doorway, she turned to Monte. "You can put the horses up. I will show this fine hombre to my casa."

"Sí." Slocum doubted that Monte enjoyed being made the horse groom. Who cared? This woman, Nada, showed him the pallet for him to sit on. When he was seated, she swept up a bottle of wine, took a swig and wiped the back of her hand over her mouth, then on her knees she pushed the bottle toward him. "Here, have some. You must be desperate."

He took the bottle from her. "Why do you say that?"

"That bastard Monte is worthless at anything." Her dark eyes glared at the door.

"What did he do to you?"

"Promised me—" She shook her head as if it was too much to explain. "I will fix you some food now." With a mad look at the closed door, she absently took the bottle and raised it for a swig again. Then she handed the bottle back to him and moved to begin building a fire in her small cooker.

"Is this your village?"

She looked up and then nodded. "I should have gone to Juárez a long time ago. There is no money here. Bandits often come by here, rape us and rob us, and the government won't do anything. They steal our young girls to sell into the slave trade."

He nodded. These simple people, farmers, woodcutters and a few miners, lived up here away from the law and its shield. It was a raw country overrun by outlaws with no respect for the people. They understood only force and the muzzle of a loaded gun.

"You have no man?"

She shook her head.

"Why do you stay?"

"How would I go? Fuck my way to Juárez? It is all I have to sell. I have no money. Then down there some mean pimp at Juárez would collar me to work for him and I'd be no better off down there than I am here."

Slocum nodded.

With a head toss to the outside, she frowned in disgust at him, "Why are you using him?"

"The wife of an amigo of mine was kidnapped by bandits. I am looking for her."

"Who kidnapped her?"

"Someone called La Cucaracha, the Cockroach."

"Ah, he is one of those bandits that raid here too." She

swung her head to indicate someone was coming.

Monte returned, opened the door, came in and took a place on the floor.

"Do the horses have feed?" Slocum asked.

"*Sí.* They will be fine. How have you been, Nada?" Monte asked.

"Fine without you."

"Ah, you have missed me not coming by to see you."

"Would you miss a large boil on your ass?"

"Oh, that is no way to talk to me. I have saved you several times."

"Ha, and you were well paid." She turned away shaking her head at his words.

"Oh, you liked it. You have any wine?" He looked around.

"You can go buy some. You have any money?"

He dropped his gaze to the blanket. "Maybe my amigo has some *dinero* and he would buy us some."

"How much is the wine?"

She wrinkled her nose. "Half a dollar a bottle."

"You know who sells it?" Slocum asked him.

"Juan sells it?" Monte asked her.

She nodded.

Slocum gave him two dollars. "Get us some wine."

Monte rose wearily, shrugged and took the money. "I'll be right back."

"Food will take some time," she said after him, tending her cooker and getting up to bar the door after him. With her back to it, she smiled slyly at Slocum.

"Quick. I seldom get such a *grande* hombre like you." She rushed over and dropped on her knees, taking his face and kissing him. Then, sprawled in his lap, she pushed her breasts into him and again sought his mouth, hugging him.

"You don't want me?" She frowned at him when he did not respond to her attack.

"Ain't that. How long will he be gone?"

"Outside?"

"No, he'll be back and interrupt us."

She wrinkled her small nose and sat up. "I thought you were a big man."

He took her face in his hands and kissed her. "Wait until he sleeps."

Looking disappointed, she rocked her head from side to side. "Oh, what a shame."

"Better undo the door," Slocum said. "He'll be back shortly."

She got up and flounced over to take off the bar. "Why do you put up with him?"

"I want to locate and rescue the lady."

"I bet he runs away when things get tough."

With a shrug, he shook his head. "He's all I have right now."

She shook her finger at him. "You must be careful."

"Oh, I will be."

In a short while Monte returned with the wine. She uncorked one bottle and took a deep drink. She handed the bottle to Slocum and he took a drink, then handed it on to Monte.

Nada made some corn tortillas and rolled up some beans and spicy sauce inside to serve them. She brought Slocum's meal first on a tray, then put some on a cracked plate for Monte. She took her place beside Slocum and drank some more wine. Fussing over him, she talked about village things— a baby was due, her cousin's second one. A man who left his wife six months ago had returned and begged her to take him back.

"Did she?" Slocum asked.

"Sure. She had no choice." She tossed down some more wine and then shook her head. "No choice. That is bad too." She shook her head again.

"When will you leave? Tomorrow?" she asked.

Monte shrugged with his mouth full. "Whenever."

"Sunup," Slocum said, not satisfied that his guide was anxious enough to get on their way early.

When they were ready to turn in, Nada told Monte he could sleep outside in a hammock. He looked at Slocum for some help.

"Don't ask me. It's her house."

Hands on her hips, she sent Monte outside, then barred the door. Then she drew a deep breath and winked at Slocum in the flickering light. Walking over to him, she unbuttoned her low-cut blouse and exposed her proud breasts right in front of his face.

"Very lovely," he said. Admiring her prizes, he handled them and kissed each one as she quickly untied the waist strings of her skirt.

"Oh, I am so excited that you are here."

She rose up and shed her skirt, then spilled on top of him before he could undo his gun belt. Quickly she sprang up and let him open the buckle and wrap the belt up. After he'd placed the gun belt close by, she fumbled with the buttons on his shirt, finally stripping it away with his vest and tenderly kissing his bare chest.

"Oh, hombre, I can hardly wait. It has been so long."

Slocum shed his boots and then dropped his pants. Now seated, she grasped his dick with her small fingers and dove for it. Her lips wrapped around his cock sent a shock wave to his brain. He kicked the britches off his feet and clutched her head as she licked and sucked on his rising appendage.

Hands under her armpits, he pulled her up to kiss her, and she was breathing so hard he worried she might have a heart attack. She wrapped her arms around his head, squeezed him against her firm breasts and in gibberish said, "Oh, oh, you are such a man."

He managed to get her underneath him, and she jack-knifed her legs so her ankles were at her ears, and he slipped his cock into her.

"Oh, oh, yes!" she cried out, hunching toward him. "You are bigger than a horse. Ride me. Ride me hard."

His world threatened to turn upside down. There was no room to spare inside her box, and the muscles clutching him were tearing at his skintight dick. The room turned into a whirlpool, and they spiraled around it like desperate lost souls until the hand of purpose squeezed his testicles so hard, he exploded inside her. They melted down like a small shard of ice in the desert sun.

"You need me to go along and help you. Your dumb, worthless guide will abandon you when things get tough. I tell you he is a liar and a sneaky coward. I know him well." Her small hand was already working on him again, and she was out of breath. He knew only another round would sate her. He kissed her.

"It will be dangerous as hell to go with us," he warned her.

She eased his rod inside her slick gates, this time with her short legs wide open for him in a wide V. "I work cheap and I know these mountains, damn good—"

6

Before dawn Slocum saddled his horse. With Nada riding double behind him, they followed Monte up the main trail. Her arms were around his waist and her tits were pressed into his back, and she seemed thrilled to be taken along. Slocum couldn't tell whether his guide liked the notion or not. But Slocum was footing the bill so Monte had little to say about who went with them.

This region was still not a part of the Madres that Slocum knew well, as he did some places on the western slopes. There were lots of pine trees at this elevation, and they spooked several mule deer that bobbed away like jackasses in high hops.

"Where are we headed?" Slocum asked when they stopped at a clear trout stream to water their horses.

"Where they have the McCarty woman."

"Good. But how come no one saw her come into the mountains?"

Monte shrugged. "I guess they disguised her as a man."

Slocum narrowed his eyes at the man. "You're certain she's up here?"

"Why would I bring you up here if she wasn't? You wouldn't pay me if she wasn't, would you?"

The man had a point, unless this Cockroach was paying him to deliver Slocum into a trap. No, Monte was too nervous to try that. Still, how did his guide know where she was hidden? Especially since no one else had seen her.

In midafternoon, they reached a village, larger than the one where Nada lived.

She leaned forward and quietly told him, "This is San Phillipe. There is a church here and a cantina. I will try to find out where the woman is. I have friends here."

She slipped off the horse's rump.

"Where will we meet you?" Slocum asked.

"I can find you, hombre," she said, and with that she was gone like a small whiff of smoke.

"Where did your *puta* go?" Monte asked.

"To see a man about a dog," Slocum said absently. "Where will we camp?"

"Oh, at a place that has horse feed."

"Good. Mine needs some good feed tonight."

"They charge more for alfalfa."

"Buy it."

Monte nodded, but seemed unconvinced. "They can eat grass just as well."

"Which would you eat, the chicken or the feathers?"

Monte simply rode on. "It is your money."

No wonder Monte had such a skinny horse. The idiot never cared for the animal. They rode over a stone bridge like the kind the Romans had built, which he'd read about in books as a boy. At the sight of some dust-coated, hipshot horses at a hitch rack, Slocum gave a head toss.

"Local vaqueros," Monte said. "That is a cantina where they hang out."

"Are they bandits?"

"Oh, maybe they ride with them—sometimes."

"We near the Cockroach's place?"

Monte shook his head.

"How much farther?"

"Tomorrow."

Slocum looked hard at the man's back. He still might need to kill him. If Monte doubted that Slocum would kill him, he better think twice. And what would Nada find in this place? She acted like she could learn something here that would help him.

The pole corrals were stout enough to hold their horses. The short, thickset, ugly man who said he owned the place asked them for twenty cents apiece to board their horses and feed them the good stuff. Slocum paid him after the man showed him a sample of the sweet-smelling hay.

When the two horses were unsaddled and put in the small pen allotted to them, Monte looked around. "Where is your *puta*? When do we eat?"

"It's still early." Slocum unrolled his bedroll and spread it out. "If she doesn't come back soon, I'll buy you something from a vendor."

"Why bring her along if she won't cook?"

"She makes good scenery," Slocum said, not interested in listening to the man bitching about her.

"She only wants part of the reward. That is the only damn reason she came along."

"Maybe," Slocum said, ready to put his hat over his face to take a siesta. "You going to guard the place?"

"I guess, if you're going to sleep."

"I'm going to do that." He rolled over onto his side, gave up on the hat and closed his eyes. Before he fell asleep, he envisioned Nada's compact body—nice.

When he awoke, she still wasn't back. He sat up and saw his guide with his back to a pine tree about half asleep.

"No problems?"

"We don't have a cook yet."

"I told you what I'd do."

"Why waste money? You brought her. She's a lazy bitch and will use you anyway to get out of work."

"Whatever." Slocum scrubbed his beard-stubbled face with his callused palms. Monte was sure pissed about having Nada along. No matter. He trusted her a lot more than he did Monte.

Maybe she would find some information he could use.

The sun dipped to touch the western horizon, and Nada arrived with two bottles of red wine and a poke full of burritos. She handed Monte one bottle of wine and two burritos wrapped in fire-flecked flour tortillas. Then she went over and sat cross-legged on the ground beside Slocum.

He opened the wine bottle and offered her a drink. With a shake of her head, she looked across at Monte. "She isn't there any longer."

"What in the fuck are you talking about?" Monte demanded.

"The hacienda woman you two came after."

"How do you know?"

"They moved her today."

"Where to?"

"You are the guide. Figure it out." She took the bottle from Slocum and then sat it on her leg and held it by the neck while she argued with Monte.

"Bitch! You don't know shit about where she is or was."

After a deep swig, she wiped her mouth on the back of her hand. "I know more than you do about her."

"Hold up," Slocum said. "First, lower your voices. Everyone in this village doesn't need to hear about our business. Second, Monte, tell me where you think she is."

"She is at a ranchero near here."

Nada shook her head. "No. She's not at the Sancho Ranchero."

"Where is she then?"

"The Cockroach moved her this morning."

"How do you know?"

"One of his men got drunk last night and told a working girl that he was taking the woman to his boss's place—this morning."

"Ha. You don't even know this boss's name. See, she has this cock-and-bull story. . . ."

"His name was Reynaldo." Her cold words made Monte stop and swallow.

"Who's he?" Slocum asked.

"Reynaldo DeVaca. He is the meanest man in this country." She shook her head. "He kills people like they were flies."

"We agree on one thing. DeVaca is a madman." Monte took more wine from the neck.

Slocum shook his head. He could not allow Martina to be in this DeVaca's hands for long, no matter if he was under another man's orders. Cruelty festered out of some men regardless of the control others had over them.

"What shall we do?" she asked.

"Either of you know where his main hideout is?"

Monte shook his head. "I only knew about this ranchero where they held her."

"Liar!" she spit out. "You don't want to remember. They told you if you ever came back they would slit your bag, jerk out your balls and stick your leg through the sac."

"Shut your mouth, bitch."

Slocum scowled at him in disbelief. "You've been to his hideout?"

"I'm not going back there. Not for any money. Not even five hundred pesos."

"Draw me a map."

Monte had dropped his head down in despair as the darkness grew deeper around them. "If those bastards ever learned I even drew it, they would find me and kill me."

"See, I told you he was a coward." Nada pointed her finger at him in disgust.

Slocum chewed on his burrito and merely nodded in reply. They had been so close, and now to discover that she'd been moved. Damn, he hated that more than anything. So close and then so far again. What should he do next?

"Why did you come?" Monte demanded of her. "Just to ruin me? Just to ruin my chances of making some money?"

Her mouth full of beans and tortillas, she shook her head at him until at last she could speak, "He would not have paid you for an empty casa."

"Stop arguing." Slocum silenced both of them. "Does this

DeVaca live on the ranchero where they held Señora McCarty?"

"I don't know," Nada said.

Monte moved closer to them. "No, it belongs to the Sancho family. They live in the federal district, and the crew of vaqueros works for a close amigo of the Cockroach."

"What's his name?"

"Ulysses."

"Maybe he will tell us where they took Señora McCarty."

"No, he is a tough hombre, and he has a dozen men." Monte took a drink from his bottle. "They are all ruthless killers."

"So?" Slocum could not believe what they were arguing about. Every bandit south of the border and most of them north would kill at the drop of a hat. His concern was not being killed but how to regain Martina from them.

"In the morning we are going to this Sancho Ranchero and see what we can learn. Now that's settled."

Damn, he hated arguments.

7

"Monte rode out last night," Nada whispered in Slocum's ear to awaken him in the cool predawn. On her knees beside the bedroll, she made a disgusted face. "I told you he was a coward. He took our food too."

"Can we find this ranch?" He rose up, propped by his elbows behind him. "We might get someone there to talk about where they took her."

She nodded firmly. "We can do anything that coward can do. And I know where the ranchero is."

"Good." He threw back the covers and pulled on his pants. "We better find something to eat."

"I know a woman who will feed us and keep her mouth shut."

"Good." He shook out his right boot to be certain no roaming scorpions had taken residence in it overnight and pulled it on. "I knew he had no backbone, but he gave up lots of money."

She shook her head. "He has no *huevos*."

He grinned at her. "You must know."

She smiled and nodded. "I know him too well."

"How far is this ranch?"

61

"A few hours."

She rolled up the bedroll and tied it with rawhide strings while he saddled the horse. In a short time, they rode out with Nada holding on behind Slocum. They took a route through the forest around the settlement and found a camp with a ramada, from which a woman emerged.

"This is Rema." Nada introduced the willowy woman who swept back her long hair.

"Good morning."

"We need some food. That snake Monte rode out on us and took the little food in our camp with him."

Rema wrinkled her nose. "That sorry prick is not worth anything."

"See? See what she thinks about him?" Nada shook her head. "She knows him too."

"Come, hombre." Rema took Slocum's hand. "I have some food for both of you."

Nada took his other arm, and the two women herded him under the ramada, which he had to duck to enter. It was a big shame they needed to get going—he could see where the three of them could have had a wild party.

Rema's food was good and spicy, but the time was short, and after they finished the meal, Slocum paid her. She stood on her toes to kiss him, then told him to come back and see her. He nodded, mounted and hoisted Nada up behind him, and they rode off.

"She is a good friend, but for a *grande* hombre like you, she would steal you." Nada laughed as she leaned over to talk to him while riding behind his back.

"Oh, no, she wouldn't do that," he teased, and she retaliated, using a soft fist to his kidneys.

The route she directed him to take certainly was a back one. It was more like a game trail than a road, but she delivered him to a place above the ranch by midmorning. On their bellies, they spied on the corral and the jacals through his telescope.

"All I see are women and a few children," he said, handing Nada the instrument.

She held the scope in both hands and agreed. "What shall we do?"

"I dislike getting tough on women. They're often just victims of their men's actions."

"They may tell us to get even with their men."

"Not likely. But we better go see what we can do."

She scooted over and kissed him. "You are serious about not hurting women. I wish there were more men like you."

He nodded and collapsed the scope, and they went for his horse. In a short while they rode inside the ranch, his hand on his hip ready to pull out the Colt if any opposition appeared.

An older woman came to meet them when they rode in. A few younger women drifted over as well, but hung back.

"What do you want here?" Her frown hooded her dark eyes.

Nada slipped off and hurried to stand in front of the horse. "We bring you no harm. We came to find the woman kidnapped from a hacienda who some men kept here."

"Look around. We have no such woman here."

Nada agreed. "But she was held here. Where did they take her?"

"I don't know what you're talking about."

"Yes, you do. She is a mother and did you no harm. Her husband wants her home."

"I don't know what you speak about." Acting haughty, the woman raised her chin and shook her head.

Nada came right back at her. "I could turn this big hombre loose on you and have him pull your fingernails out by the roots to help your memory."

"Who are you?" the woman demanded.

"I am not important. Look at your hands. How much pain is in store for you?"

"She is not here. They took her away yesterday morning. She wanted to be with her lover."

"Who is that?" Nada asked with a frown.

"The one who kidnapped her."

Nada turned to Slocum, who was looking around. "You hear her?"

He turned back to face the woman. "La Cucaracha has her?"

"*Sí*, señor. We had nothing to do with them holding her here."

He drew a deep breath. *Her lover?* Why would she think that about Martina?

Martina was a rich woman living with a man who was a great provider. How in the hell could she be under the spell of some worthless bandit? He couldn't believe his own ears.

"Surely you are mistaken about her affection for this bandit?"

The woman swung around, and the three younger ones standing back nodded in agreement with her.

One of them spoke up, "Señor, I heard her ask the men to take her to him."

Still shocked, Slocum wondered why they lied so well. "Ask her where this one hides out," he instructed Nada.

"Where is this Cockroach at?" Nada said sharply.

"Sierra Vista," the woman said, like it was no secret.

Nada turned for Slocum's response. He knew that town. Taking the information under consideration, he nodded. "Tell her *gracias*."

"Is that all we need?" Nada asked. When he told her yes, she ran for the horse and brought it to him. He mounted, then caught her arm and tossed her on behind him. He saluted the women, and they left the place.

"What do you think now?" Nada asked when they were out of earshot.

"I find it hard to believe that Martina had taken a lover like him."

"Lots of women have been led off by some worthless hombres."

"But she has a son she seemed to adore, and she was always so loyal to her husband."

Nada hugged him and put her cheek on his back. "I am sorry we heard such bad news."

"You wish to go to Sierra Vista?"

"With you?" She squeezed him tighter.

"Who else?"

"Of course. I would ride to the end of the world if you would take me."

"We'll go to Sierra Vista. I have friends there who will put us up."

"Good," she said, acting like an excited young girl.

"Why did no one know the Cockroach had been up there?" he asked and reined his horse around a small landslide on the mountainside.

"I never heard anyone say he had been there before that woman told us."

Lots of new information had turned up. Most was different than he expected or than he ever dreamed—he still wasn't taking it all for fact. He booted Baldy into a trot.

8

In a small village that Slocum and Nada passed through, Slocum bought food from a vendor and then rode on to a place along a gurgling stream. There in the sundown, sitting cross-legged on the ground, they ate their burritos and talked about Sierra Vista.

"You have never been there?" he asked Nada.

"I have never been far from where I live. I am a coward, no?"

"Many people never leave where they were born. They aren't cowards."

"Oh, you say that to please me."

"No, when they come out of the womb, they are planted in that place."

"I never heard of that before."

When she finished eating, she brought him some water in a tin cup to wash down his food. Then he straightened his legs and she sat on his lap.

"Who are you, hombre? You speak good Spanish, but you are no Mexican.

"I am from America. We had a big war, a terrible war, a long terrible war. At the end it changed everything for me."

"No woman? No babies? No casa?"

He turned her face toward his and kissed her. Her hands sought his face and clung to him, their mouths sipping honey and fire. In search of her womanly source, his hand slid under her skirt and over her smooth, short legs. She widened her knees for him to explore. When his finger penetrated her, she moved her butt closer to him. He played carefully with her clit until it at last stood erect.

Her red face and rapid breathing told him all he needed to know. His arms under her legs, he swept her up and took her to the bedroll. When he set her down, she shed the dress and he toed off his boots. She tore open his pants and dropped to her knees. Her hand, twisting and pulling on his erection, soon had his pump primed, and she responded by taking his tool into her mouth. The instant her hot tongue touched the sensitive skin on his dick, a bolt of lightening shot to his brain. He clutched her head, and she took most of the length down her throat. Her efforts churned his stomach and he wanted to dance on his toes to escape her attack. Her mouth and tongue soon made his head swim even more.

He came and she rose up with the white foam dribbling from both sides of her mouth. "Oh, you are wonderful."

In moments they were in the bedroll, and like a serpent she had rolled under him and stuffed his erection inside her pussy. He went for his prize, pounding her ass between her raised legs with a fury. Their world spun on a fast axis until excitement pulled his trigger. His balls cried out when he fired another volley inside her.

They collapsed in a pile, still connected. She eased him out and rolled over, cuddling up to him like a spoon. He replaced his dick inside her, and she reached back to clap his bare hip.

"Thank you, my lover."

Sometime in the night, he woke and discovered they were still attached and moved to go in deeper. His actions roused her, and she reached back to help him get closer. "Mother of God—I can't believe it. Oh, please don't quit."

Dawn was a small purple light coming over the mountain when he rolled her over and gave her another good breathtaking romp from the top.

A short while later, sitting in the saddle, he hoisted her up behind him. Eating some crackers and jerky as they rode on their way, they talked and laughed about nothing in particular.

In midafternoon they rode up a backstreet in Sierra Vista. High-walled estates lined the stone street. Bougainvillea vines and red flowers cloaked the walls, and a familiar gate stood open. Slocum rode in and a gray-headed, straight-backed woman came to the doorway.

"Slocum," she said. "We were not expecting you."

"Shush, lower your voice. No one else is either."

She laughed like a woman caught in her own joke. "Juan, close the gate and take his horse. We have a guest, and he brought us a pretty lady."

He swung the beaming Nada down onto the stone paving. "Nada is her name. Nada, this is Donna."

"Oh, Slocum," Donna said. "It has been a long time since you visited us. What brings you here in vaquero clothing to this casa?"

"A friend's wife was kidnapped, and in the attack he took several bullets and one cost him his arm. So since he is healing—I am looking for his wife."

"And you, Nada?"

She shrugged, still looking around, impressed at the sprawling flowers and opulence of the place. "I am only his helper."

"You are very pretty. He is fortunate to have such lovely company. Come into the house. I will feed you, then if you wish we can draw you a warm bath and let you rest. The *patrón* will be home late tonight. He went to the mines to see about some timbers they need."

"I trust he is all right?"

"Don Carlos is fine. He will be happy to see you," she said to Slocum.

"I need to know about this bandit, La Cucaracha. He's the one who kidnapped my friend's wife."

She shook her head. "He is not in Sierra Vista. Who said he was here?"

"Some women we talked to in the mountains. They said some men took the kidnapped woman here to that man."

Nada nodded to back his story.

"We can ask Don Carlos, but I believe those women lied to you. Come eat and then have a bath." She looked Nada over. "I have a fresh dress that will fit you too."

"*Gracias.*" Nada made a curtsy for her.

"Nothing is too good for this hombre." She clapped Slocum on the arm.

"I agree, Donna. I really agree," Nada said.

Later, taking a bath, Slocum still felt lost. First they said that Martina went to her lover in this village. Then Donna, who knew so much about the town, said the bandit wasn't here. Damn, he was chasing loose ends and still niggled badly about the Martina's lover story.

Time would tell. Someone came into the bathroom when he stood up. Nada attacked him with a towel. "I think you need to be dried off, hombre."

"Oh, I need a new brain."

"What is your plan?"

"After dark I am going to scout around and see what I can find out."

"I want to go. I have never seen a real town."

"It could be dangerous."

"I'm pretty streetwise for a country girl."

"But it will not be a place to let down your guard."

"I won't."

"All right, but I warned you."

She fussed with drying off his privates and then looked up at him. "Why have I not known you all my life?"

"I don't live in the Madres." He pulled her up and kissed her hard on the mouth.

"Oh, I knew this would be fun, but not so much."

"We better get ready for supper."

"Oh, Donna found me this wonderful dress. I won't look like the *puta* from the mountains wearing it."

He spanked her on the ass and sent her off.

In the front room, Slocum drank some of his absent host's whiskey and waited. Donna came in and said they were still fixing Nada's hair. He smiled and thanked her. "When is Don Carlos coming in?"

"You know men, they get involved. With women sometimes, and business the rest of the time."

He nodded and grinned at her words. He'd known this woman well enough over the years, from the large mole beside her twat to the scar on her shoulder where a jealous lover had once tried to carve her up. Donna was a generous woman who took care of her boss and his amigos. She was a good administrator for Don Carlos too. Slocum was surprised that Don Carlos had not married her by now. But when it came to women, Don Carlos was a butterfly flitting from flower to flower, like some others he knew.

When the delighted Nada joined them, with her hair in great curls to her bare shoulders, she looked like a rich man's wife. His approving smile made her blush. Donna decided they should eat. There was no telling when her truant employer would get there. The milk fat lamb was delicious in mint sauce. The enchiladas were baked to perfection and her hot apple pie was mouthwatering.

"I am so full I may burst," Slocum said.

"Good. He's such a vast hombre to fill," Donna said privately to Nada.

She agreed.

After Nada changed back into her traveling clothes, she and Slocum left the casa and moved on foot through the streets to the square. A band played in the center on a raised stand. The good horn player's snappy renditions carried across the dancers under the Chinese lanterns. Mexican people were raised on dirt floors and they could dance on that surface too.

A handsome young man came over and politely asked to dance with Nada. He bowed to both of them politely, and Slocum told her to go ahead. At the edge of the crowd, Slocum looked over the shadowy faces for someone familiar. He saw no one but kept up his search of the crowd. After the song ended the young man returned Nada and thanked him.

"His name is Salazar. Mendez Salazar. He must have money," she said.

"He doesn't plan to take you to meet his grandmother, does he?"

She gave Slocum a feigned punch in the side. "He was polite and well mannered."

"Listen close. Someone here knows Martina's whereabouts."

"Oh, I am listening." She made Slocum dance with her next, and he saw a man in the crowd with a long scar on his left cheek. He should know that hombre—where did he know him from? They swirled around to the music and he lost sight of Scar Face.

"Did you see someone you know?" Nada asked.

He gave her a sharp nod, and she pressed her small body against him again.

At last at the edge of the crowd he led her back a step or two into the shadows.

"Who was it?"

"A man with a bad knife scar on his left cheek. I should know him."

She shook her head that she didn't know anyone like that. "Salazar is coming back."

"Learn what you can."

Pleasantries were exchanged, and Salazar led Nada away to dance some more.

When she returned, she told him that Salazar had offered her ten pesos to spend the night with him.

"What did you tell him?"

"I am not for sale. Was that all right?"

"You don't need to do that for me."

"Good, I will sleep with you then. He must be very rich to offer so much money for one night, no?"

"He made a generous offer."

"Maybe I should live here."

"Maybe, but what if he invites four horny bucks over to share you with them?"

"That would be bad."

"Let's move around the square. I want to see this Scar Face again."

"Certainly." She took his left arm and they eased through the looser crowd on the outside. They passed by sour-smelling batwing doors and on toward a cantina where the crowd was loud and the piano music tinny and bad compared to the band in the square.

Slocum held her back. He was able to see Monte up ahead with his back to a porch post. They detoured and stepped back to observe him.

"Did you know the man with him?" she whispered when Monte and another man walked away.

"No."

"His name is Cordova. He is a cattle buyer. I wonder what they are doing?"

"Does Monte work for him?"

She shrugged. "I don't think Monte ever works."

"Wait." Slocum caught her arm. "That man smoking the cigar in the doorway of the cantina ahead. See him? He is a pistolero who once worked on a hacienda I stayed at."

"What is his name?"

"They called him—I'll think of it in a minute. Oh, yes. His name is Flores."

"What should we do?"

"Buy him a drink as though we want to hire him."

"I should go along?"

"Sure."

He led her to the cantina's door, and the man looked at them at first as though he didn't know Slocum.

"Pardon, señor, but isn't your name Flores?" Slocum asked.

The man frowned at him. "Where do you know me from?"

"A hacienda in Sonora where you once worked. Are you employed now?"

"No. Do you have work?"

"Let's go in and have a drink. We can talk in there about it."

"Sure. You know my name. What is yours?"

Slocum tossed his head toward the side of the smoky room. "Find us a booth, and we can talk there."

The man agreed and turned on his heel to lead the way.

At last in a side booth, Slocum introduced Nada and then told Flores his name.

"Ah, *sí*. I remember you. You are the gringo."

Slocum nodded. "You know this hombre called the Cockroach?"

"To know much about him is a death wish." Flores shook his head.

"You know where I can find him?"

The man drew in his breath. "Why? Do you want to die?"

"He kidnapped a woman—the wife of my good friend—and left my friend shot up, so I am looking for her."

"What do you need me for?"

"Information."

"You don't understand. To even speak of him out loud, they will cut your throat."

"Who are his men?"

"Mother of God, I only know a few, but he has spies all over."

"Is the man with a knife scar on his left cheek one of them?"

"Cicatriz."

"Means 'scar.' Is he one of them?" Slocum placed a ten dollar gold piece on the table and slid it with his index finger across the table toward the man.

Out of the tops of his eyes, Flores looked warily at him. "That could cost me my life."

"Yes or no?"

"*Sí*, but there are others who protect this one."

"Why?"

"He pays them well."

"How many?"

Flores shook his head.

"If this man is so secret, how did he raise such a large army to attack my friend's hacienda?"

The bar maid brought them draft beer in tall mugs and Slocum paid her.

Nada rose up on her knees in the booth to drink hers and to listen closer to them. Before they started back in about the Cockroach, she asked Flores about Mendez Salazar.

"Son of a rich banker in Mexico City. He is here looking for excitement. His father is so important no one would touch him. A wild, crazy boy." Flores discounted him with a shrug.

"What if he knows something?" she asked Slocum.

"Too dangerous."

She gave a shrug and raised her mug. "So no one will give us the information of who he is? This Cockroach?"

Flores nodded. "It is best not to mention him, for if his protectors hear you are asking, you can be in the alley in the morning with your throat cut."

Slocum agreed. "Someone knows who he is, but it won't be easy to find out."

"What should we do?" she asked.

"We'll look into it in the morning."

"Do you have work for me?" Flores asked.

"I want him," Slocum said, under his breath. "We must be careful. You listen around tonight. I will meet you at the horse auction Saturday. I saw a poster on it."

"It is a big event." Then Flores sipped his beer.

"I understand many horse buyers come from a distance to attend such an event. Until then, cover your tracks," Slocum said to the man and fiddled with his beer mug. "Anyone asks, I am a horse buyer for a rich man in Nogales."

"I am certain, señor, that you will find some fine horses there."

Slocum raised his voice too. "*Gracias*, señor, for your time."

Obviously Flores wanted someone to hear them talking business. Slocum shoved his untouched beer across the table for Flores to drink. "Good to meet you. See you at the sale, and maybe you can deliver those to the man for me if I buy any."

"Ah, *sí*, señor. And to you, my darling, *gracias* too."

Nada nodded at him.

In minutes they were headed up the narrow street for Don Carlos's casa. A block farther along, Slocum pulled her into a narrow alleyway and then listened.

"Someone is coming," she whispered.

He nodded and drew his gun. When the person went past them, Slocum stepped out behind him. "Stop or I'll shoot you."

"Huh?"

"Shut up and get in the alley."

"What do you want, señor? I have little money."

Slocum shoved the man's face into the wall and jerked out the man's handgun from its holster, then handed it to Nada. "Who are you?"

"López, Ronaldo López."

Slocum suspected that was a lie. "Who do you work for?"

"I just do work for anyone who will hire me."

Slocum shoved him harder against the wall. "I don't like your answers. You want your throat cut and your friends to find you in this alley tomorrow?"

"No."

"Start over. Who are you?"

"Lou Reyes."

"Better. Who do you work for?"

"A man hired me."

"What man?"

"I don't know him."

"Bullshit. You must know everyone in this town." Slocum shoved his face hard into the wall.

"Oh, you broke my nose. His name is Vasquez, or something like that."

"Who does he work for?"

No answer.

"Does he work for La Cucaracha?"

"I don't know him."

Slocum slammed the butt of his six-gun down onto the man's right shoulder. The man cried out sharply as the blow drove him to his knees. He began sobbing.

"Shut up or I will cut your throat. Does he work for the Cockroach?"

"*Sí.* Don't hit me anymore."

"You know that when he finds out you told me, you are a marked man."

Between sobs, the man said, *"Sí."*

Still gripping a handful of the top of his shirt, Slocum shoved him facedown on the ground. "Then you better go find or steal a horse and ride out of here or else you will be dead. And if you follow me ever again, you really will die."

"Oh, my shoulder is broken." The man moaned, gripping his shoulder with his hand.

"Better than your throat cut. Now get out of town."

"I am going. I am going." The man crawled on the ground until he figured he was far enough away not to get struck again, then he climbed to his feet and left, holding his right arm to his chest.

"You get a look at him?" Slocum asked Nada.

"Not a good one, but he was nobody."

"Tracking us." He took the man's cap and ball pistol from her and stuck it in his waistband. "Let's get going. I think that is all the company we'll get tonight."

"I hope so. That scared me to death."

"You have lived a sheltered life in the mountains. In this village men are rough on *putas* for no reason at all."

She nodded that she heard him. When he looked around, he saw only the staggering coward who had been trailing them as he hurried away toward the square. The coast looked clear, and they left, walking quickly, for his amigo's casa.

There were many things going on in this place. Slocum simply did not have them all figured out. If they were holding Martina here—where exactly was she?

9

An armed man cracked open the gate for them. In the shadowy light, his face opened as he recognized Slocum. "Donna said you'd be returning tonight."

"Thanks. Is my amigo Don Carlos back yet?" Slocum asked.

"No, and I think she is upset that he is not here. She is awake in the house."

"Gracias."

"She must have been expecting him," Nada said, close at his side as they moved along the walkway in the light of a few Chinese lamps.

"We'll ask her," he said under his breath to her.

She agreed with a nod and went inside the house with him.

"You are still up?" Slocum asked when Donna sprang from the chair.

She swept her salt-and-pepper hair back from her face. "I must have fallen asleep. Did you learn anything?"

"Oh, bits and pieces. You are concerned about Don Carlos?"

She made a peeved face. "Oh, I always worry about something. But he usually rides in when he tells me he will. Sometimes a day later." She made a face that showed she understood about the distractions there were for men and continued, "He was due here twenty-four hours ago. I said nothing because, like I said, he can be detained."

"Where did he go?"

"To check on some mining operations is all he said."

"He has several of those?"

"Yes, and some partnerships as well."

"If I went looking for him, where would I start?"

For a second, a flush of concern crossed her face. "Oh, he might get angry with me if I sent you up there."

"I can save you that. Let me catch a few hours' sleep, and then I'll ride up there and see about him."

She chewed on her lower lip and at last agreed.

"Get me up in four hours and I'll go see if I can find him."

"*Sí.* I really am concerned."

He hugged her shoulder. "I'll find him."

"Over breakfast I will have Chavez tell you where we think he went."

"That would help. Get some sleep."

He knew she wouldn't, but it sounded good anyway. With Nada under his arm, Slocum headed for their room. When the door was closed behind them, she stood on her toes. "*Gracias* for taking me with you tonight. I wish I could be more help to you."

He hung up his holster on a hat tree, watching her unbutton her dress before him in the flickering light. She let her dress fall to the floor, and then she stepped over it to hug him. "You be careful."

He kissed her, toeing off his boots. "You are hard company to leave. But stay here at the casa and be careful. They could find out you are with me and might think you know something."

"I will be here. Do you have time for us?"

His pants off, he swept her up. "Of course." He dropped her on the feather bed, then shed his hat and shirt. "I always have time for you."

"Ah, hombre, you are the one." She scooted the covers out

from under her back and kicked them to the foot of the bed, holding out her arms for him to mount her.

"I need nothing but you in me," she whispered. "That is like lightning to me."

He saddled himself in on top of her and found that she was ready. The gates were already lubricated for him, and she raised her butt off the bed to accept all of him. Her arms wrapped around him, and she squeezed him inside and out.

"Oh, oh, my hombre, you are too good to be real. . . ."

Slocum was locked in sleep when someone knocked on the door a few hours later. He rose, still fuzzy-headed, to sit on the edge of the bed, and Nada tackled him from behind. "I am coming to have breakfast with you."

"Good. It might brighten my day."

"Oh, I could do that."

"Sorry. Don't have time." His pulled on his pants and his boots.

She laughed. "I know, I know."

"You stay right here. This is a safe place."

"Oh, I will. I will."

"Good."

"I know you have been thinking about this one they call La Cucaracha. Who is he?"

"Kind of like smoke, ain't he?"

"No one talks about him either."

Slocum agreed. It had him puzzled. Most Mexican chiefs of movements and armies were very apparent. This one was unseen, and they kept it that way by killing anyone who spoke out about him, or even asked.

Slocum and Nada hurried through the hallways to breakfast. Donna was standing there prim and proper, just as he expected. She had never slept a wink.

"This is Chavez," Donna said. "He can tell you where we think Don Carlos went."

"I can ride with you, señor," said the man, who looked to be in his forties.

"No, this place must be secure first. I can find Don Carlos, unless the earth swallowed him."

Chavez nodded and blew on his coffee. "He was to go to the Ruby Mine first and see about some problems they are having with timbers."

"I know that mine."

"Then he mentioned the mine in Oro Canyon."

"He having trouble there?"

Chavez shrugged. "Have you been to that mine?"

Slocum nodded his thanks to the girl who brought his heaping plate of breakfast. "No, but I have been to Oro Canyon."

"From this direction, after you get to Oro Canyon it's in on the right about halfway to the trailhead that goes out of the Madres."

"The one they use for hauling ore-loaded mule trains to Silver City, New Mexico."

"*Sí*, you can't miss it."

"*Gracias,*" Slocum said and began eating his breakfast.

"I have put some jerky, ground corn and brown sugar mix in your saddlebags, some raisins, extra matches, a slicker and a thin bedroll wrapped in canvas, a small axe. Is there anything else?"

"Canteens?"

"Two filled with water."

"Sounds wonderful," he managed between bites.

"I hope he comes in today," Donna said.

"So do I. Chavez, tell me what you know about this outlaw, the Cockroach."

"I hear a few things." The man shook his head. "But I don't know who he is. Maybe he is two or three men."

"Whoa. You think he's more than one person?"

Chavez turned up his callused palms. "I have wondered about it."

Slocum turned to Nada. "What do you think?"

"Makes good sense, huh?"

"Yes, why didn't I think about that before?"

She shrugged and grinned. "You had not got that far."

They all laughed.

The Ruby Mine was four hours or more away. When he left the village under the stars, Slocum made certain no one was following him by reining off the road and waiting in a turpentine-smelling grove of pines for fifteen minutes or so. Then, satisfied no one was trailing him, he trotted the bald-faced horse to the north. Out of nowhere, Angela's abrupt departure and McCarty's three ranch hands waiting at St. Francis came to his mind. There still were some days left before he had promised to get back to them. Perhaps they had learned something more about this Cockroach.

The Ruby Mine took its name from the man who first discovered the gold vein. Don Carlos came in as an investor, and Ruby made enough money to sell out and go live in Veracruz with some *putas* in a fancy castle. But Ruby's transition to a settled life had been a little bumpy. He'd lived too long on the wild Mexican frontier to really become a part of that rich society. Besides publicly scratching his crotch when it itched, he'd once whipped his dong out to show some very fancy ladies what they were missing by not having an affair with him. One was the wife of a very high official in the government. She had fainted at the sight of his huge dick, then, behind her husband's back, started calling her husband "Little Peter." But last Slocum heard of him, Ruby threw his own parties and the fancy folk avoided them.

Slocum spoke to the mine superintendent, a man called Vincennes, who told him that Don Carlos had ridden on to the Oro Canyon operation two days earlier. After thanking him, Slocum headed out. Oro Canyon was a good ways farther up the road, but he pushed on and arrived at the front gate in the middle of the night. A sleepy guard with a rifle refused him entrance and told him to come back when the mine was open.

Slocum swung around on Baldy and headed back south. After a quarter mile, he turned off the road and hobbled his mountain horse out of sight, then made his way around back under the stars and came in on the small buildings that were the offices for the mine. He tried the back door of the main office and discovered that it was unlocked. In the starlight coming through a front window, he saw three people bound and gagged on the floor.

"Don't make a sound," Slocum whispered, using his jack-knife to cut the woman loose first.

"Oh, I am so glad you found us," she whispered hoarsely as she shook the rest of the ropes loose.

"What happened here?" he asked, busily cutting the bindings on the second person, a young man.

"Several men took over the mine four days ago. They began to load two pack trains of mules with rich ore over the last two days, and today they set out with it."

"*Gracias*, señor," the young man said.

"How long have you been tied?" Slocum asked.

"A day anyway," the young man said, heading for the door.

Slocum jumped up and caught him. "You can't go out there. Where are you headed?"

"I've got to piss!"

"Piss in the corner over there. She won't look." Slocum looked at the woman for a confirming nod, then continued, "There're still damn guards they left here."

The third man, after he was untied and the gag was taken from his mouth, looked obviously shaken in the poor light. He bore a wound where someone had hit him on the forehead—possibly with a piece of pipe or a gun barrel—and the blood had dried on his face.

"Where is Don Carlos?"

"I think at my casa," said the older man, who was apparently the mine boss.

"Keep your voices down."

The older man agreed and then shook his head as if all was lost. "To be sure, they are already over the pass with those mules and gold. It's too late to stop them."

"Lead the way to the house. We must find Don Carlos first before we worry about that the ore. Do either of you have a gun?" he asked the younger man and the woman.

"There is one in the desk drawer," the woman said. "It is loaded. I don't think they took it."

Slocum told the younger man to get it. She went instead.

"Can you use a gun?" Slocum asked the young man.

The man swallowed hard. "I am not sure."

"I can," the woman said.

"Good. Take out that guard down at the road. I don't care if you shoot him or whatever. Then hide, so if there are more of them, they won't find you."

"Where are you going, señor?" the woman asked.

"Me and the boss are going to find Don Carlos. Alive or dead."

"Oh, I hope he is all right."

"I hope so too. Be quiet and take that guard out. Then you must hide like I said," Slocum made clear to them.

"*Sí,*" they replied. Then the woman and the young man left the office and headed toward the gate.

Slocum and the older man headed for the casa. There was a light on inside the residence, and they stole up alongside the building. Slocum, with his .44 in his fist, got to a window and could see the bedraggled-looking Don Carlos tied up in a high-backed wooden chair. Thank God he was alive.

"Untie him," Slocum told his companion and went to find the outlaws.

There was a pistol shot behind them from the direction of the gate, then another. Two men he had heard talking beyond the door jumped up and ran to the front door.

"Delo, what's going on?" one of them shouted.

"Put your hands in the air or die!" Slocum ordered, slipping into the room behind them.

The second man spun and took a shot at Slocum, but too late. Slocum's shot caught him with a lead bullet in the face. The other man tried to charge back into the house, but his falling buddy blocked the doorway. Slocum rushed over to cover them.

Slocum jammed the muzzle of his Colt to the man's temple. "I'm counting to three, then I shoot you. Tell me who you are, who you work for and where the others are at. One—"

"Ricky Carmella. Ricky Carmella. My boss is—my boss is Andrew, and he is gone with the mules."

Slocum ripped the man's gun away and then looked up at Don Carlos, who was taking ropes off his hands as he stood in the doorway.

"Ah, amigo," said Don Carlos. "Why did it take you so long to get here?"

They hugged each other.

"I came as soon as I thought you had finished your business with some sweet thing and needed to be back at your casa."

"Soon enough. Soon enough." Don Carlos dropped his chin, and at the sound of the woman's voice, his head flew up. "Clara?"

"That guard bastard down there won't rape anyone ever again." She rushed over and hugged her boss. "You are all right?"

"I'm fine, my darling. Give me that gun," Don Carlos said, holding her tight. "You may shoot one of us waving it around like that."

She handed him the revolver.

"Where are the other men?" the older man asked, looking around.

"Locked in the mine," Don Carlos said.

"Where are the women and children?" Clara asked.

"They put all the families in the warehouse," Don Carlos said to her and his mine superintendent. "Ralph, have you met my amigo, Slocum?"

"Yes, he untied us."

Slocum shook Ralph's hand.

"How did you ever take them on by yourself?" Ralph asked.

Slocum shook his head. "They were down to three guards, who were obviously buying them time for the pack trains to get out of the valley."

"How far away are they? Do you think they have gotten away with the ore?" Don Carlos asked.

"Somewhere between here and the pass up north would be my guess," Slocum said.

"No way to stop them." Don Carlos dropped his chin in defeat.

"Do you have some tough men working for you?" Slocum asked.

"Yes, but—"

"Go get them out of the mine. Are there any horses or mules to ride?"

"Sure, but—"

"We need them. We'll need saddles and guns." Slocum's mind was rolling out the things that he needed to make up an army.

"The guns are in the supply room," Don Carlos said. "There's ammo too."

The young man, no doubt an accountant who couldn't shoot, came over with an inventory book. "What all do you need, señor?"

"Blasting powder, blasting sticks, detonating caps—let me see. I'll need some bows and arrows."

The man dropped the book down against his legs. "We have none of them."

"These mountain people work in your mine?"

"*Sí.*"

"They will know all about them. They'll find some." Slocum thanked him.

Inside of an hour, Slocum had assembled a dozen good riders, men who could ride and shoot. They carried saddlebags loaded with blasting sticks. Two of them had made crude bows and short arrows.

Outside the ring of lamps, Slocum spoke with a man Don Carlos introduced as Indio, a hard-faced man with lots of Indian blood in his veins.

"Can we take another route and cut them off at the pass?" Slocum asked him.

"*Sí*, señor, but it is a difficult and dangerous path, and not all of us who take that trail at night will live, I fear."

"Tell the men of the danger. I want six to go and try to head them off. Tell them how hard and bad the ride will be before you ask for volunteers. You must cut them off from the pass and send them back to us. Shoot blasting sticks at them. Kill anyone who does not turn back. I figure they will be up there at the pass near dawn."

In his deep, rusty voice, Indio said, "All right, I know the men I need. They will follow me. They hate these men for raping their daughters and wives when they were here loading the mules."

Slocum nodded his approval. "They deserve to die."

"They will," Indio promised him.

"We will come up the trail from behind them and cut off any retreat."

"*Vaya con Dios,*" the man said.

Slocum agreed and sent the man on his way. "You wish to wait here?" he asked Don Carlos.

"Hell, no. I want all those bastards killed and I want to help do it."

"Get a horse for both of us then. Mine is tired."

"Ralph! Two good horses," Don Carlos shouted and waved his arms as though to bring on an army.

Two stout horses soon appeared. Don Carlos called them to come over, then he turned to Slocum. "Why are you here?"

"A bandit called La Cucaracha attacked my friend McCarty's hacienda and kidnapped his wife, Martina. McCarty lost his arm and has two bullets in his back so I came up to find his wife. Someone said they had her at a place in Sierra Vista, but they had moved her when we got up there. You were late getting home, so I came to look for you. I will have to get back to looking for Martina and the Cockroach soon, though. Do you know anyone who has ever talked to or seen this one they call La Cucaracha?"

"I should have known you are doing good for people," Don Carlos said and shook his head. "My God, this has been a nightmare."

The man continued, "You can find no one who has seen

La Cucaracha because he is a ghost." He shook his head. "There is no Cockroach."

"But they say he leads them." Did Don Carlos really know?

"No, his men get his orders and they follow them. He is never there."

Indio came by with his armed men all on horseback. He spoke in a strong voice. "Be ready, *patrón*. We will send them back to you."

"God be with you, hombres," Don Carlos shouted, and the crowd cheered as the men tore away in the night.

Slocum stepped up onto his horse. Don Carlos followed him, and they trailed Indio's band up the road. Behind Slocum and his friend rode two dozen armed men ready to meet the wave of mule trains that he counted on Indio turning back. Only time would tell if the plan would work.

"We need to be at the base of the pass to catch them," Don Carlos said as they rode side by side.

Slocum agreed. Dust was churned up by the horses' and mules' hooves. Slocum's belly rubbed on empty. This was a desperate business. Some of the men were to take a deadly shortcut in the darkness. If Indio and his crew failed to turn the bandits back, there would be no recovery of the ore. The boiling dust stung Slocum's eyes. Up ahead, Indio and his men soon took their leave from the main trail and disappeared into the night.

Slocum led the second column with Don Carlos. Since he was in the lead, the stirred-up dirt wasn't as bad for him as for the men in back. They trotted their animals when the terrain let them. A jingle of metal, the protest of their saddles, mules and horses snorting out of their nostrils and men's coughing filled the night. The dark junipers along the way looked like giant squat frogs. No moon overhead made their progress slower than Slocum would have liked.

Hours later, he heard a mule up ahead braying away and halted the column. "Keep our mules quiet," Slocum ordered. Men jumped off to muzzle their animals, but not before several had brayed.

"What is it?" Don Carlos asked him.

"That may be them. They may have put off climbing the mountain till daylight," Slocum said. "Everyone get your guns. Tie your animals good or we may have to walk back."

"I can hear them," Don Carlos said. "There are many mules up there."

"You're right—"

Shots rang out in the night, and Don Carlos was struck by one. Slocum ran over in time to cushion his fall off the horse. Another miner rushed in to help him, and they carried Don Carlos to cover. Bullets whizzed all around like angry hornets.

"They may try to charge us. Spread out and lay down some fire," Slocum ordered. "How are you doing?" he asked his friend.

Don Carlos, his teeth clenched, managed, "Hurting like hell."

"You have any liquor?" Slocum asked the man on Don Carlos's other side, who was using a folded sleeve torn off his own shirt to press on the wound.

The man shouted over his shoulder for some liquor. The miners' bullets were taking effect on the bandits. Wounded men and mules were screaming in the night. A man running low to reach them delivered a bottle to Slocum.

He raised Don Carlos's head and the other man, Ramon, fed him some of the liquor, mescal or tequila, probably. The pack train bandits had stopped shooting, and Slocum felt they were either about to run away up the mountain or charge back through them.

"Amigos," he shouted "be ready! They may try to break through us."

The thunder of hooves told him he had correctly guessed their plan.

Anger must have powered them. The miners rushed to block any opening and fired the repeating rifles from the mine armory in a constant barrage. Horses, mules and riders went down. When their magazines were empty, the miners, armed with knives or their bare hands, tore the bandits from their mounts to stab or beat them to death.

"Any get by?" Slocum shouted over their war cries.

"One or two got by us," one man responded.

"Three or four of you head back for the mine so they don't harm anyone there."

"There are three of us who have guns and animals to ride," a man shouted. "We will take care of the mine and the families."

"Be careful. They're butchers," Slocum shouted back. "How many of our men are wounded?" he asked the first man who brought a lighted torch.

"Not many," the young man said.

"Good. Bring those who can be moved over here—carefully."

Shortly, several of the men began collecting loose horses and mules.

Four men who had been wounded lay beside Don Carlos, some of whom were only slightly injured and would be able to ride back under their own power. Things were shaping up. Several mules with packs still on them were being gathered. Two dead miners were located, and their bodies were brought to Slocum's command post.

"We need some long poles to make ambulances between two horses or mules to transport Don Carlos and the other badly wounded men back to Sierra Vista."

"Hell, I can ride a horse," Don Carlos protested.

"No, you can't," Slocum said, loud enough that all the men nearby heard him. Others tending the wounded nodded their approval of his observation of their *patrón*'s condition.

"There is a corral down the road," a young man said. "It has some good rails in it."

"Borrow them. We can pay back the owner later."

The man took some others and they raced off to get the rails.

"I'm not a baby," Don Carlos protested.

"No, but it is important that you live," Slocum said.

"Seven wounded outlaws," a gray-haired man with a rifle reported, driving his wards into Slocum's central command area.

"Find out about their boss. Who they work for."

"What if they won't tell me? They're being pretty close-mouthed."

A big, burly man from the mine stepped up, armed with a machete. "Which one won't talk to you?"

"Him, for one."

The knife-wielding man put the sharp edge of his instrument to the man's chest. "How many fingers do you have?"

"Ten."

"No, now you will have nine. Put your hand on that log."

Bug-eyed, the outlaw shrank back. "What do you need to know?"

The big man gave a head toss to the interrogator. "Ask him before I chop his whole hand off."

"Who do you work for?"

A silence spread over everyone. Except for the raucous braying of some mules, the valley was shrouded in quiet.

The man barely managed to say, "La Cucaracha."

Slocum pointed at him. "Who is he? Tell us who he is!"

The man shook his head and shouted out loud, "I don't know! I never met him."

With two hands on the machete handle, the big man slashed off the outlaw's left ear alongside his face and the blood flowed freely. "No more lies! Tell us."

"Mother of God!" the gang member screamed, holding the side of his head with his hand. "You have killed me. I have never seen him. Only the big bosses see him."

Don Carlos, lying on a blanket, nodded at the stone-faced Slocum standing above him. "See? It is as I told you."

No one had seen him—yet he led many gangs.

Unbelievable.

10

Slocum caught a young man by the sleeve. "Take a fast horse. Ride to the mine. Get another fresh horse there and ride like the wind to Sierra Vista to Don Carlos's casa. You know where he lives?"

"*Sí*, señor."

"There is a woman there named Donna. Tell her to get a doctor and meet us on the road coming to town from Oro Canyon, and that we are bringing her Don Carlos, who has been wounded."

"Tell her to bring me some good whiskey too," Don Carlos said and closed his eyes.

Slocum gave the boy a slight shove to hurry him on his way. "Be quick about it."

The racket of someone dragging poles sounded good to Slocum as the mine foreman further interrogated the outlaws seated on the ground. The man in charge of the pack train recovery reported to them that he had recovered all but three mules.

"That is good news," Slocum said to Ralph, who was to be in charge. Then he went to check on the conveyances that were to take the three worst injured, including Don Carlos, to medical attention. In the first light, he could see many of the

92

men had lesser wounds and were busy working on many projects. But he couldn't miss the pride on their faces.

"We don't have enough mules," a man said when he joined those making the ambulances.

"Go tell the men to unload some of the ore and use those mules. Lives are more important than gold."

"*Sí*, señor."

Slocum found his own horse tied with a few others. He led him back to the central command.

"They are unloading some mules," Ralph said when he joined him.

"Good. Don Carlos, you all right?"

The solemn man nodded from the pallet. He cleared his throat, "I am fine."

"Liar," Slocum said with a grin. He turned back to Ralph. "Are the mules coming for the ambulance?"

"*Sí*, señor, and I will need a few men to ride with that train," Ralph said.

"Will you need me?" Slocum asked.

"No. We can handle it. I have sent for food and help from the mine."

"Do you think we have all the gang? How has the interrogation gone?" Slocum asked.

"We know a man named Tonto Silva got away. He was one of the leaders of the gang and the most hated one for what he did to many of our women during the time they held the mine to get the ore."

"We'll find him," Slocum said. "Who else?"

"There was a madman called the Bad One that we cannot find. He strangled everyone with his huge hands, anyone who objected to their actions."

"Have we learned anything about La Cucaracha?"

"No one knows him by his face," Ralph said. He called to his man, and the gray-haired interrogator came over. "Slocum asks about La Cucaracha."

The man nodded. "These men are peons. We have none of the leaders. They escaped."

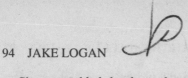

Slocum nodded that he understood. This was the case in many such incidents. The real bad ones sneaked away.

"Señor, they are ready to go with the wounded," a young man shouted.

After giving Ralph a firm handshake, Slocum told the man to keep up the good work. They carefully loaded his friend Don Carlos in the conveyance, and Slocum mounted his horse, thanking all who could hear him. A cheer went up and he waved, riding beside Don Carlos, who was in a swing between two mules.

Before they reached the mine, several *carritos* loaded with food and more help for the others stopped, and a woman handed Slocum two tortilla-wrapped burritos. A man gave him a bottle of red wine.

"*Gracias*. The rest of the men need this too," he said.

"Should we use one of these wagons to haul the wounded?" a man on horseback asked him.

"No," Slocum said. "This is easier on them than a *carrito*."

Don Carlos was eating when Slocum rejoined him.

"Food for a king," his amigo said.

"I thought I'd never eat again," Slocum said and laughed, grateful for every bite.

Several woman and children were standing beside the road that led to the mine. They had rosary beads in their hands and many were on their knees, praying for Don Carlos and blessing him.

Don Carlos managed to sit up and nod at them in passing. The sad thing was that one of the wounded men had died on the trip back. They were down to two ambulances carrying wounded men. Slocum, concerned about his friend's weakening condition, made them continue on. Time slipped away, and he grew more anxious about Don Carlos's wound going untreated and the complications that might result.

A bit before noon, they met the conveyance bringing the doctor and Donna, who came from the surrey with her dress hem held high as she raced to where Slocum dismounted to stand beside his friend.

"How is he?" she asked, out of breath and still a few feet away from seeing Don Carlos.

"Looking for the whiskey he asked for."

"Aw, hell with his whiskey. How is he?"

Don Carlos opened his eyes and smiled for her. "I'm—fine."

"You don't look fine to me," she snapped, and everyone laughed. Then she stepped aside for the doctor and shook her head. "He's as loco as usual."

Donna motioned for Slocum to come over and spoke under her breath. "You should know. Nada left the casa last night and was not back when we left."

"You know where she went?"

Donna shook her head.

"When I am certain Don Carlos is under the best care, I'll go see if I can find her."

She agreed. "What is his wound?"

"I think his shoulder, but I have no idea about the damage. He was shot very early on and has scoffed at it."

"I know him well. We can transport him and the other man in the surrey back to the hospital or the casa, whatever Dr. Carmichael wants."

"He is in good hands then. I will ride into town and look for Nada."

"Check at the house first. She may have returned."

"Is this Friday?"

She nodded.

Good. The horse auction was still a day away, and he needed to reach his pistoleros, who were waiting for him in St. Francis, as well.

"You look tired," Donna said.

He nodded that he heard her. "I will go on since you are here to look after Don Carlos."

She clapped his arm. "*Gracias* for all you have done for him."

Slocum acknowledged her words, mounted his horse and loped off for Sierra Vista. What in the hell had Nada gotten herself into? At Don Carlos's house, he found that Nada was still absent, and the women in the kitchen fed him. He told them what he knew about their boss man's wound. Grave-faced, they politely left him to eat his food.

After his meal Slocum headed for the square, and when he hitched his horse at a rack, Obregón walked over, shaking his head. "We heard you were up here and came to find you rather than wait in St. Francis. We still know very little about this one, the Cockroach. He hides well."

Grateful to see his pistolero, Slocum agreed. "I have been up north at a mine robbery. A woman who was helping me here has vanished. Her name is Nada."

"What does she look like?" Obregón grinned at him.

"A short Mexican woman—" Slocum gave up and went to shake hands with the other two men, who had just arrived.

"The Apache don't know of this man Cockroach," Cherry-cow said with a grim set to his mouth.

"I think he is a ghost," Slocum said.

Jesús frowned at him. "I don't want to mess with him then."

"Let's go inside and have a cerveza." Slocum waved them inside the cantina, and they found a table in the back.

A young barmaid came by and sat on Obregón's lap. "What will you hombres have?"

"Four beers."

"Nothing else?" she asked.

"What do you have to eat that is not rotten?"

"All our food is fresh." She acted insulted.

"Bring us some frijoles and tortillas for my amigos."

She looked at Slocum and then nodded.

"Wait," Slocum said. "There was a girl named Nada who may have come to the square last night. She never came home."

"Was she this short?" Then she tucked the tray under her arm and showed off a set of tits over twice her size with her hands.

"Yeah. Where is she?"

She looked around, then leaned her elbows on the table. "I

think she is fucking Mendez." With a shrug of her thin shoulders, she rose up, hugging the tray. "But who knows, huh?"

Slocum nodded and understood what she meant.

Obregón looked after her. "What did she mean by that?"

"She's with this Mendez. A man she met night before last here at the fandango."

"Will you go look for him?"

"After you all eat your frijoles and drink your beer."

The three grinned in approval and raised their mugs to salute him.

"What do you really think about this Cockroach that no one knows?" Jesús asked.

"It may be two or three men hiding behind that name. Then they send out their men to do some crime. No one knows who it is, but I think there is more than one main leader responsible for these raids."

Obregón shook his head. "At the hacienda, we heard he was a big, sword-waving generalissimo. But he never came with those raiders to the McCarty Hacienda. All that night I thought, where is this bastard?"

"I wondered too. Where is he hiding? I just came from a raid on one of my amigo's mines. The peons who were the bandits said it was the Cockroach's raid, but they didn't know him either."

"So who is La Cucaracha?" Jesús asked. The pistolero looked at him very seriously between spoonfuls of the hot beans.

"I think it is a committee that makes the plans for these raids."

The three nodded between feeding their faces and swigging down their second beers. Slocum felt his three men were worth an army. Somehow he needed to find an answer to the source of these bastards, these bandits. And they might even now be sitting only a hundred feet from those leaders. But the very next problem for him was to find Nada. Was it a coincidence that she was still gone, or had she learned too much somewhere? The second possibility concerned him.

Mendez Salazar—Slocum would need to talk to him.

Sashaying over to Slocum, the bar girl leaned on his shoulder, pressing her small breasts into his arm, knowing he was the one paying for their meal. "Were the beans good?"

"They said so." He lowered his voice. "Where can I find Mendez?"

"Oh, he has an apartment down on Agave Street."

"You been there?"

She wrinkled her nose. "*Sí*. He thinks he is a great lover."

Slocum nodded. "Where exactly is it at?"

"Above the saddle shop."

"Does it have a back entrance?"

"Some stairs. The one time I went to his place, he sent me down them so some big, important visitor wouldn't know I had been there. They are painted green. They are the only stairs that are green."

"What does that back doorway open into?"

"A hallway."

"What else should I do to get in there?"

"I guess go knock on the door."

"Will he answer it?"

"I guess so."

"What else can you tell me?"

She cupped her hand over his ear. "I think he has problems."

Slocum frowned.

"His dick won't get hard. You know what that means? He blames the woman who is with him for that. When I learned that, I knew I was lucky that he put me out that day before he tried me and I sure never went back. Such a man blames you and he might kill you. Huh?"

"I see. What is your name?" Slocum asked.

"Sudsy."

"Why that?"

She laughed and blushed. "I used to wash the dishes back there." She gave a head toss toward the back room. "They said I was too skinny to be a barmaid."

"Nice to know you, Sudsy." He put the money for the meals and beer and on the table and gave her a silver peso.

"*Gracias.*" Then she gathered up the mugs and dishes. When he stood up, she bumped him on purpose with her hip. Everyone laughed as they went outside.

"Where do we go next?" Obregón asked.

"To see if Nada is in Mendez Salazar's apartment."

Obregón looked around the square when they were outside. "What if she is not there?"

"The search continues." Slocum told Obregón and Jesús to wait in the alley and watch the green stairs for anyone coming down them.

"Cherrycow and I will knock on the front door."

The two pistoleros nodded and walked away like their business was over.

"You like to live in this place?" Cherrycow asked, looking around with distaste written on his dark face.

"Nice place to visit," Slocum said.

"Maybe—but so many live here. Hard to find a place to piss."

Slocum laughed and told him to go between the buildings. He watched the man who had lived in two worlds go find a place to empty his bladder—what a problem. No private place to piss. He looked down the street and saw the saddle hanging on the sign. In a few minutes he'd know if Nada was up there.

11

Slocum and Cherrycow took the stairs beside the saddle shop that led to a closed door at the top of the landing. The grit on their soles made a quiet, sanding sound on the already worn boards. At the top, Slocum softly tried the knob—locked. He flattened himself to the wall, away from the door knob, and waved for Cherrycow to get down a few steps. Then he reached over and knocked. Waited, no answer. He shared a nod with his partner. Then he reared back and used his right boot to smash the door open.

Six-gun in his fist, Slocum saw no one in the first room, then stepped inside and waved for his partner to come in. Cherrycow carried his pistol at the ready. There was a messed up, unmade bed in the center of the room, a couple of old stuffed chairs, some empty wine bottles on a table. The two front windows were open, and the dirty lace curtains waved in the breeze. A foul smell pervaded the room despite the open windows.

The place stunk of an unemptied chamber pot. Slocum moved across the bare floor, which creaked under his soles. As he headed for the back door, he tried a side room door. It was locked. Then he walked to the back door at the end of the hall. That door wasn't locked and he opened it. He nodded to his two men in the alley, who quickly came up the stairs.

"Anyone here?" Obregón asked, looking over everything in the neighborhood as he climbed the stairs.

"No. I can't tell when they were here last either."

The pistolero wrinkled his nose at the smell when he reached the entrance. Slocum took the key left in the back door and went down the hall to the locked door. With a turn of the key, the door opened. A small, dirty side window let some light in the room. On the floor was something wrapped in a blanket. Slocum knelt down and began to unroll it, knowing full well the wrap contained a body.

He closed his eyes when he saw the messed hair and bloody face—Nada.

"Is it her?" Obregón asked over his shoulder.

"Yes." Slocum could hardly swallow. His eyes squeezed shut, he rose, went to the back door and puked over the side of the landing.

"What can we do here?" Jesús asked.

"There must be police in this town," Slocum said.

They agreed.

"But they might be in with this Cockroach gang too," Obregón said.

"We have to take a chance that they aren't. I want you three to go and stay at Don Carlos's casa. I'll meet you there later. We will close this place up, and I will go report it to the police."

They agreed again and shut the front door, and all of them went out the back way. In the alley Slocum told them the directions on how to get to the casa, and they parted. A man in the square directed Slocum to the jail.

A large man wearing a badge, with dusty shoes propped on the desk, and no socks, sat snoring in the chair at the jail.

"Señor." Slocum waited in the doorway for him to respond. Sometimes lawmen, jarred from sleep, thought they were under attack, drew their gun and shot someone. Slocum was taking no chances on this one.

"Huh?"

"Are you the police?"

The man blinked at him. "Why are you waking me up from my siesta?"

"A woman has been murdered."

"Who?"

"A woman named Nada. I don't know her last name."

"Where is she?"

"In an apartment off the square."

The man rubbed his unshaven face with his palm. "Who in the fuck are you?"

"A good friend of Don Carlos. My name is Slocum."

The man sniffed a *hmm* out his nose, did not offer his own name. Then, waving his right hand with a "come on" sign for Slocum, said, "Why did you kill her?"

"I didn't kill her. I found her."

"Was she a *puta*?"

"What difference does that make? She was a good person. No one had the right to kill her." His patience had worn thin.

"If you didn't kill her, who did?" He put both shoes on the floor and made a face like it was all lots of work.

"If I knew that for certain I'd already have killed him. Do you want to see the body?"

"Hell, yes. I am the law here."

"Good."

The man strapped on a short-barreled Colt in a gun belt around his flabby waist. Then he jammed the revolver down in his holster like he feared it might fall out. He combed his unkempt black hair back with his fingers and put on a wide black sombrero, making the chin string tight.

"Go on. I will follow."

By this time, Slocum was fed up with this lackey's slovenly ways and set out for the square. In half a block the man called him back, out of breath and coughing. "You go too fast."

"You go too slow," Slocum replied. The policeman, his elbow leaning on the plaster side of the building, heaved for his breath. Coughed some more. "No rush. She's dead, isn't she?"

At this point Slocum didn't answer. The lawman made two more stops to catch his breath on the way to Salazar's apartment, then at last he looked up the stairs in disgust. "There better be a body up there."

"There is."

"Mother of God, why couldn't you have waited for me to have my siesta?"

Slocum never answered him.

"Who else was up there?"

"No one but her when I found her."

"This your place?"

"No. I'll go up and wait for you."

"Whose place is this?"

"I think Mendez Salazar's."

"No, he is the son of a very rich man. Why would he have such a dump of a place as this?"

"They told me in the cantina he rented this apartment."

The man waved Slocum's answer away. "They lied to you, señor. I know this man well."

"The body is upstairs." He started up and let the man come up at his own speed. Once up there Slocum sat on a wooden chair, listening to the policeman huff and cough his way up.

"Where is this body?"

"In the back room on the floor."

"Show me."

Slocum rose while his companion hacked up more phlegm and spit it on the floor. "Go ahead."

He opened the door and let the man go inside the room. The lawman knelt down beside Nada's body and then nodded. "Why did you kill her?"

"Damnit, I found her here thirty minutes ago."

The man with great effort rose and folded his arms over his chest. "You found her up here and you thought she had fucked someone, so you killed her."

"Are you deaf? I didn't kill her. I found her like this thirty minutes ago."

"You broke down the door when she would not answer and came in here and killed her. Men do it all the time all over Mexico every day. They get angry and then kill the *puta* for being disloyal."

"Why would I come and get you if I killed her?"

"Why not? So the town would bury her for you, huh?"

"She's been dead for hours. I was bringing Don Carlos, who was shot, down from the mountains all last night."

"Hmm, who shot him?"

"Some of the Cockroach's men who were robbing the Oro Canyon mine."

"That is the best story I ever heard in a case like this."

"Check with Don Carlos."

"I will. You are under arrest for the murder of this *puta*—what was her name?"

Slocum jammed his Colt into the man's belly and took the policeman's short-barreled pistol away from him. "I don't have time to mess with you, you son of bitch. Get your hands up. Where are the keys to your handcuffs?"

Hands raised, he said, "I don't need any keys."

Slocum found the handcuffs open in the man's back pocket. He clamped one on the man's right wrist and the other to the door knob. That would hold him for a while.

"You can't do this! I am the gawdamn law!"

Before he left the man, Slocum took the short-barreled Colt out of his pocket. He emptied the revolver of the cartridges and wondered where to throw it. "You can have your siesta now."

"You can't do this! I am the law."

"Well, practice it." Slocum was gone. At the foot of the stairs, he tossed the six-gun in a pile of trash and began to run. He was maybe a half mile from Don Carlos's casa.

If his friend was sleeping, Donna would know what to do—or he'd simply get out of town. That fat slob wasn't jailing him for Nada's murder. A block away, he could still hear the fat man's faint shouts for help. A woman came by him in a small buggy going down the street.

"Wait. Wait," he called to her, and to his surprise, she stopped.

Out of breath, he managed, "My good friend Don Carlos was shot last night. I need a ride to his casa right now."

"I know him well," the woman said. "Get in. I'll take you there."

With a sigh, he sank onto the horsehair-stuffed leather seat beside her. "I'm sure mighty pleased. Thanks a lot."

"Any friend of Señor Carlos is a friend of mine. My name is Minnie Stallings."

"Nice to meet you, Señora Stallings. My name is Slocum." He noticed she was dressed in black. Must be a widow.

She sat on the seat, very straight backed, and from the looks of her clothing, not poor by any means. With the reins, she slapped her fine sorrel buggy horse on the butt, and he set out at a swift trot. Nice rig for a place like this. Skillfully she guided the horse around potholes and watched for the naked children at play who might run out in front of the buggy.

"How is Don Carlos doing? I mean, will he be all right?"

"I think so. But it was a long ride back from where the bandits shot him."

"Did you bring him back?"

"I was part of that team."

"I don't believe I have ever met you before."

"No, I don't recall you either. I am usually on the move when I come through here and visit him."

"Well, perhaps if he runs out of room sometime and you are passing by, you could stop at my casa. I don't get a chance to speak English with very many people up here, and it is nice to talk with someone in my native language."

"Yes, ma'am. It is nice to ease back into your first language. Have you lived here long?"

"About five years. My husband, Harold, died two years ago of a heart attack. I had the casa and the money he invested here in the mining business. So I decided I would stay, since we had no children and my parents are deceased."

"I see."

"What sort of business are you in, sir?"

"Right now I'm looking for a friend's wife who was kidnapped. They took her in a raid on his hacienda. Left him without an arm and with several bullets in his body, so I am looking for her."

"My, my, that is a grim task. Have they asked for a ransom?"

"That is another concern—my knowledge now is they have not." Ahead he could see several *federale* soldiers dismounted in the street before Don Carlos's gate. He reached over and put his hand on her wrist.

"Ma'am, I don't need to talk to those gentlemen. Let me out here."

She turned the horse around smartly. "You need a place. You can stay at my casa, and I'll find out why the military is here."

"I'm not wanted by the *federales*, but they can question you for weeks if they incarcerate you. I don't have that time to waste."

"I understand perfectly. Get up, Tony. We're going home, boy."

Mrs. Minnie Stallings's dwelling was no simple adobe quarters. They passed through a guarded gate and went up a limestone-paved, twisting driveway lined with flowers to a large stone-and-beam house. A young groom came and politely took the horse. Checking the sun time as they walked under the apple trees, she remarked that they probably needed lunch and invited him inside.

"I didn't come to impose on you," he said, giving the girl who greeted them his hat. Slocum had already had a small meal at Don Carlos's casa, but that was a couple of hours ago now, and he could certainly eat again.

"My dear," she said to the girl. "Slocum and I will be dining on the patio. See they bring him adequate food, and I will have my usual fruit salad."

"Yes, ma'am." The girl curtseyed and left them.

On the patio, Minnie uncorked a bottle of wine and turned to Slocum. "Would you rather have good whiskey?"

"I never turn down good whiskey. There isn't much of it in Mexico."

She reached into the cupboard that stood countertop high and brought out a square bottle of whiskey, then set a crystal glass in front of him. "Pour your own poison."

He did and then he toasted her glass of wine. "Here's to your hospitality. *Gracias*."

"Here's to your stay as well."

He considered her slender hips. How old was she? Early forties, perhaps older, he thought. A well-preserved woman, and she wasn't as haughty and cold as she had first appeared to him in the buggy. They sat on cushioned chairs that one sprawled in, and lunch came on trays the servants set up beside their lounges.

Slocum noted that Minnie's plate had fresh fruit: sliced peaches, cut up melons, cherries that were pitted and red bananas. His platter bore several pieces of sizzling-hot flank steak with red sweet peppers and onion slices cooked with it, as well as hot pinto beans in a small pot and several fresh-made flour tortillas. He nodded his approval to the server.

"Smells delightful," he said. His mouth flooded with saliva at the prospect of what lay ahead.

She soon shortened the distance between them by moving closer—food and all. Then she began to feed him small pieces of her fruit with her fingers between his own bites with a murmured, "Try this."

He could hardly believe the transition of her attitude toward him. From aloof buggy driver to generous hostess—he was getting excited about the change in her attitude.

She drew closer and closer, hand-feeding him until he moved her finger aside and kissed her sweetly on the mouth. At that point she scooted over to the very edge of her seat, and when he went to kiss her again she threw her arms around his neck and he tasted an anxious woman's mouth. Then, without effort, she moved over to share his chair, pressing her hip against him with the crinkling sound of the material in her driving dress.

She pulled her face free, seeking her breath, and slumped in his arms. Then, toying with his neckerchief knot with her fingers, she said, "Some like to take siestas. Others while that time away. But before we get too involved anymore here, get your bottle and I'll get mine, and we shall retire to my more private quarters."

"Thank you, ma'am. You lead the way, my lady."

"Should we send a message to your friend that you are safe?"

He made a face and a head shake that neither was necessary.

Hugging his arm, she wore a victory smile as she led him through the hallways to a palatial room in the rear. She swept back the silk goose down cover and sheets.

He felt the cool chill in the back of the great house where the sun had not yet warmed it. He toed his boots off, removed his gun belt and, after rebuckling it, hung it close by the bed on a high-backed chair. She began unbuttoning her dress. Her fingers shook, making it difficult.

"Is it cold in here?" she asked.

He moved in closer and agreed that it was. Sweeping her up in his arms, he kissed her. His right hand molded her breast. Her eyes squeezed shut, she completed all the buttons that she could reach and shrugged out of the dress. They swept the camisole off over her head, and she shed her slip off over her ankles. Within moments, his shirt was gone, and he shoved the leather britches off his hips. Her slender, snowy hips swaying, she led them to the bed, and once both of them were on the mattress, she swung the goose down comforter over them. She pressed herself against his body, squeezing her hands and shaking from the coolness.

His strong arms hugged her to him. Like a small flame in a stove, the heat from their bodies began to grow in their cocoon. As the minutes passed, Slocum felt confident that they would recover from the chill.

"Oh, how foolish of me," Minnie said in soft, shaky voice. "I could have let the whole world see me naked over ruining this moment like I did. I never dreamed it would be this cold in the back bedroom."

"Hell, we've got all day." His finger touched her lip. "No problem. We can do anything we wish. A little delay doesn't hurt anything."

She closed her eyes with her arms between them and her hands clasped. "Oh, I wanted it to go so smoothly."

He rocked her. "It will be. It will be."

"A crazy old woman . . ."

"You're lovely." He began to smother her with kisses. In response, she raised her rump off the sheet and opened her knees. Her eyelashes squeezed tight shut, she froze rigid. When he pushed his stiff dick between her gates, her mouth formed an O, then she relaxed and collapsed with a sigh of relief.

The excitement of their coupling fully aroused her. She began gasping for breath and tossing her head, lost in the fury of their passion. Arching her back to receive all of him, their coarse pubic hair began to rub the skin raw between them. Then he felt a twinge in his scrotum and slammed himself deep in her tight cavern for a big explosion that caused her to faint.

"Oh," she said dreamily, coming to from her faintness. "I didn't ruin it after all."

He kissed her hard. "Not at all."

Snuggled against him, she laughed. "Who says you can't have fun?"

"Not me. Not me."

After darkness fell, Slocum kissed his generous hostess good-bye at the back door and slipped off for Don Carlos's casa. Using the dark backstreets he made his way quickly through the cool night and let himself in the back gate, which was unlocked. In the kitchen, he asked for Donna, and a young girl went to get her. He refused the offer of food and took a glass of red wine. Donna came running through the door and blinked at him. "First the *federales*, then the police were here looking for you!"

"I know. Someone murdered Nada, and that worthless policeman accused me of doing it. I found her body in someone's apartment, and when I took the policeman up there, he wanted to arrest me. So I shucked him."

"He came here with three officers. I don't know why he chose us."

Slocum could see she was upset. "I'm sorry they upset you. How is Don Carlos?"

"I wish he were better." She stood before him, looking ready to cry.

"What can I do to help you?" He stepped in and hugged her.

"Nothing. He is in God's hands." She sobbed on Slocum's shoulder. "Oh, what will I do if I lose him?"

"He's tough as an oak. He'll pull through. Where are my men?" he asked her.

"Here," Obregón announced, stepping from the doorway into the kitchen. "We have been waiting for you too. Glad you are all right."

"Any word on this man Mendez Salazar?" Slocum asked him.

"We've learned more about how Nada was with him last night and went to his apartment with him."

"Who told you that?" Slocum asked.

"Two *putas* we met after we left you. They are afraid they may be his next victims."

"Where is this Salazar?"

"No one knows. He is a shadow. His father is a very rich man in Mexico City, and his son comes and goes like a ghost."

"He's damn sure not a ghost. Nada danced with him the night we came here, and he offered her ten pesos to sleep with him."

The other two joined him and Obregón. "You two learn anything else about this Salazar?" Slocum asked.

"I think he has a large casa west of town. Perhaps he is hiding out there," Cherrycow said.

"You mean the Cortez House?" Donna asked.

Jesús agreed. "*Sí*, it is a big estate."

"Could it be part of his family's holdings?" Slocum asked her.

"I never thought about it as some kind of hideout." She squeezed her chin. "But it always has had a strong presence of armed guards around it. If you have nothing to hide, why have all those armed guards around the place?"

"I agree." Slocum turned to Cherrycow. "Can you shoot a bow?"

He nodded matter-of-factly.

"Make one and some arrows. You two help him. We'll need lots of rope and several blasting sticks."

"Monterrey Mercantile has all that. Don Carlos has an account there," Donna said.

"Obregón, you go down there. Get two cases of blasting sticks, fuses, cord. Does he need anything special in order to put that on Don Carlos's bill?"

She shook her head. "I can send a note to them that you are his special agent."

"I can take that," Slocum said.

"What about the police?" she asked.

Slocum shook his head. "They are not swift enough to cut our trails."

Jesús agreed.

After Slocum and his men spent four hours loading blasting sticks, creating some rope scaling ladders and making a bow and some arrows, Slocum's complete setup for the raid was concealed under some straw in a *carrito*. Jesús, dressed in peon clothing, drove an old mule they rented to pull the cart to the area of the big estate, while Slocum and the other two scouted around, planning to meet him there later in the night.

Near midnight, after evaluating the guard situation, they crouched on their haunches and discussed their strategy. On a hillside close by the mansion's stark silhouette, which was outlined by the light of a half moon, they spoke in low voices.

"I think those guards have grown lazy," Obregón said. "Who would want to raid this estate anyway? There are much easier pickings to be had robbing banks and stagecoaches that carry real money. So why have so many armed men around the place?"

"I figure we will learn the answer once we are inside," Slocum said.

"I think we can open a door in the back. Screw those guards," Obregón said, scoffing about the men in uniforms who carried single-shot rifles. Only the captain, who they had seen ride toward town earlier when they were on the road, even had a pistol on him.

"Tell us about this door you saw," Slocum said to Obregón.

"Every walled hacienda has one. They are escape hatches if it gets too bad inside. This one is old and looks weak. Two or three of us ram it good, and it will crash inside."

"Everyone carry their weapons and blasting sticks, plus the rope scaling ladders. We may need them to get out of there. Any questions?"

"What are we trying to find out in there?" Jesús asked.

"We first need to know who that building is hiding and why."

"*Sí.*" Jesús acted satisfied.

"Can we have the money we find?" Obregón asked.

"If it wasn't freshly stolen from someone, yes. But don't forget that Martina McCarty may be in there too. I don't want anything to happen to her."

"Ah, *sí.* She is our grand lady too."

Obregón was right about her.

They soon stood inside the courtyard with the rotten doorway barely hanging on by one rusty hinge. Slocum sent the two pistoleros to the right, while he and Cherrycow went left.

They took out a sleepy guard, then bound him hand and foot and jammed his mouth full of a rag to gag him.

Moving on, they let two gossiping women go by them as they hid in the shadows, and when the pair went into a side room, two of his men moved out of the shadows and inside the casa. At the foot of the stairs, the four men gathered.

"See anything?" Obregón hissed.

"Just that one guard we gagged and tied up," Slocum said. "I'll go upstairs and check it out."

Pistol in his fist, Slocum took the steps two at a time. On the second floor, he began to search. The first room he opened was empty. In the next bedroom, there was a woman sleeping in a curled-up fetal position. A small candle lighted the room. Slocum stepped closer to see if he knew who she was. Not Martina. He eased out and quietly shut the door. He kept close to the wall so no one would see him from down on the first floor. The next door was locked.

He went to the third one. The knob twisted and the door barely squeaked as he eased it open.

"Drop the gun, señor."

A pistol muzzle jammed against his ribs, Slocum let the pistol in his hand fall to the floor with a clunk. A trap. He'd walked into a damn trap. How had they come to expect him? At once he realized that they had killed Nada to draw him to this place. *The sonsabitches.*

"I have been expecting you, señor. I imagine by now my guards have captured your men downstairs as well."

"Well, Salazar, what role do you play in this opera?" Slocum asked, recognizing the man.

The man about broke up laughing. "Opera? What opera?"

He went back into his hilarious laughter. "That is—I can't get my breath—so damn funny."

"Is Martina here?"

Salazar shook his head. "No, she is not here, nor is her son."

Slocum about blinked. Her son? They said they had hidden that boy at the hacienda, and they told him the bandits never got him. Had they gone back and kidnapped him too? Damn.

"We have a fine prison in the cellar where you can rot until I figure out what I want do with you. You might be worth some ransom from your amigo McCarty. Get going, and don't try anything."

"You taking ransom for his wife?"

"Oh, no. She is so loving and caring and such a damn good piece of ass, I'm not letting him have her back." He stopped at the head of the stairs, his pistol pointing at the two pistoleros with their hands on their heads, surrounded by Salazar's guards.

Where was Cherrycow? Had they killed him? Damn, Slocum had slipped up badly, not giving Salazar enough credit. The son of a bitch had murdered Nada so he could catch Slocum. Salazar turned him over to his guards.

"Lock them up. We'll see if their employer will pay a ransom for them. If not, we can feed them to the hogs.

"Oh, Slocum," Salazar continued, "when I see Martina again, I will tell her not to worry about you rescuing her." His laughter echoed down the hallway.

The four guards roughly hustled the three of them down the stone stairs into the dank basement and then shoved them into one of the iron-barred cells. The man with the mustache and big girth laughed when he locked the door. "Sleep tight, you fucking gringo."

The three of them alone at last, Slocum turned to the pair of pistoleros. "They didn't get Cherrycow."

Obregón shook his head. "No, he must have gotten away. He slipped out on them—somehow."

"He's still an Apache," Slocum said. "He may be our best chance to get out of this piss-stinking prison."

One flickering candle lamp was all they had for light. "Either of you have something I can use to pick the lock?" Slocum asked after searching his own pockets.

Both men shook their heads.

"Salazar told me he had Martina's son too."

"No." Jesús scowled over the information. "There is no way he could have gotten that boy."

"Damn funny, but the sumbitch said that to me upstairs."

"Why would he tell you that?" Obregón asked.

"I don't know, but he sounded to me like he's screwing the ass off Martina McCarty, and she's really giving her all."

"He is a blowhard. Martina McCarty is a lady." Obregón smashed his fist into his palm. "I will personally castrate that worthless dog when I get out of here."

"That won't be easy." Slocum rattled the barred door. "If we get out of this door, there are two more they closed going out of here."

"Think of something. You are a smart man," Jesús said.

"Smart, maybe, but this is serious business, and we're in up to our necks in this prison."

Before long, the candle lamp outside the cell burned itself out, and they sat in total darkness—waiting.

Hours later, a bent-over old man brought a pail of beans and some dry corn tortillas. Three guards armed with rifles and carrying lamps accompanied him, and they kept a close eye on everything. It was all tough business. The prisoners were ordered to the back of the cell by the riflemen. Then one of the guards unlocked the door for the old man to set the bucket on the floor along with the tortillas.

"We need some water," Obregón said.

"Drink your piss," one guard said, and Slocum had to catch Obregón's arm to restrain him.

"When we get time we will bring you some," the guard in charge said.

The door was relocked. They did leave a candle lamp to replace the one that went out, but the light was still dim in the cell.

Slocum listened to them locking the other doors and going upstairs. They had one hope—somehow Cherrycow had gotten away.

"Obregón, you can't lose your temper with those armed guards. We have no gun, no weapons. Control it and pray for help."

The man nodded his head.

The three seated themselves on the stone floor around the bucket and fed their faces. The stale tortillas were hard enough to use for scoops, and they dipped out the nearly soured beans with them. Slocum knew that despite the poor quality of the food, they had to eat something until help came. The other two, after complaining, must have accepted it as their fate as they feasted with him.

No telling the time or how long they had been there, but their confinement grew tedious on all three of them—maybe on Slocum the most.

12

Slocum hissed at the other two. He heard the sound of shoe soles descending the stone steps. Someone was coming. It was not the sound of the guards' heavy sandals this time; that's what made him sharpen his senses. The candle lamp had long since gone out again, so there was no light in the room.

"Think it is Cherrycow?" Jesús asked in a whisper.

"Time that bastard got here," Obregón complained.

The outer door to the jail chamber opened with a weary creak. Whoever was over there hissed, "Slocum, you in here?"

A woman's voice, one he recognized in the inky darkness of the cell. Slocum was surprised, but thankful it was her.

"Yes, I'm here. Is that you, Angela?" He frowned in disbelief. How had she ever—?

"*Sí.*" She fumbled with the key in the lock.

"You have no light?" Obregón asked as the three men joined her at the locked cell door. At last the barred door opened and they were free.

"Do you have a gun?" Slocum hugged her shoulder in the darkness.

"*Sí*, two, and they are loaded." It was pitch dark and she reached for Slocum's hand to give him a revolver, then she handed Obregón the other one. "They were all I could get."

"What time is it?" Slocum asked.

"Maybe three o'clock in the morning. I am unsure."

"Lead the way. Everyone put their hand on the next one's back. Let's go," he said.

"Oh, *Madre de Dios*," Obregón said. "I am so grateful to you for this."

They passed through the next door and climbed the steep steps. Slocum saw some light ahead and felt grateful too. "Are there still a lot of guards up there?"

There was enough light that he saw her shake her head.

"What has happened that you got in here to let us out?"

"The captain of the guard. He was horny."

Slocum asked no more as they stepped into the hallway. Even though it was dim, the light was almost too much for the three men.

"Follow me," Angela said and led them out into the back courtyard.

With his bow strung over his shoulder, Cherrycow stood up and waved at them to follow him.

"Where in the hell have you been?" Obregón demanded, looking around.

"Busy trying to get you out," the man spoke brusquely. "That is not easy. Angela was the one who found you. I was in that casa three times since they caught you, but I couldn't find you."

"We were in the prison underground," Slocum said.

"Juan, the old man who took you your food, told me where you were," Angela said and then pointed to the waiting horses.

"Why did he tell you that?"

She smiled in the starlight as they reached the picketed horses. "A woman has ways to get information from men that even torture cannot get from them. Even really old men."

He did not need any more answer than that. They checked their cinches and then mounted up. In the saddle, Slocum reached down and hoisted Angela up behind him.

"Can we go to Don Carlos's house and rest?" Slocum asked Cherrycow.

"*Sí*, he was very worried about where you were when you did not come back."

"He doing better?"

"Much better."

"That's good news."

As they rode away, Slocum looked back at the outline of the huge, fortified building. What really went on inside that house?

"Whatever brought you back?" he asked Angela in a whisper.

"Oh, we can talk about that later. Just a witch's way. Keep going." She booted the horse they shared to make him go faster.

"You learn anything about the operations inside that house?" he asked her.

She hugged him around the middle, driving her breasts into his back. "I think it houses La Cucaracha."

Slocum looked back and frowned at her as they crossed over a good-sized hill, the mountain horse under him hunching his way up the grade. "He's in there?"

"I think his operations are in there."

"Not him?"

"I think the one who is him may be calling himself something else."

"I've thought that for a long time," Slocum said. Had she really found out who the Cockroach was?

"Has anyone ever seen him?" Slocum asked her.

"No. I think whoever is playing him is like an actor in a play and uses that house to hide his identity."

"It could be anyone then, huh?"

"I asked *el capitán*, but he told me nothing. But I think it is all some scheme so if his house of cards falls down, La Cucaracha can escape and not be sought. You can't arrest someone when you don't know who you're looking for, right?"

Slocum agreed. After they were well away, they stopped briefly to eat some dried food that Cherrycow had in his saddlebags—Slocum and the two pistoleros were ravenous since the food they'd gotten during their confinement was terrible, and they'd had to force themselves to eat enough to keep their strength up.

They reached Don Carlos's house a couple of hours later, and Slocum's friend looked fresh sitting in a lounge chair, just finishing his breakfast.

"I see you made it out all right."

"Thanks to one brave lady—Angela," Slocum said and indicated her.

"*Gracias*, my dear. You have saved my great amigo, who in turn saved me and my ore from the bandits," he said, starting to rise.

"You look very good." Slocum shook his hand and made him stay sitting down.

Slocum squatted on his boot heels. "Salazar said Martina McCarty wasn't at the house. Have you heard anything about where they have taken McCarty's wife?"

"Who is Salazar anyway?" Angela asked.

"Mendez Salazar. He runs that operation at the house, or at least he acted like he did. He's the one who killed Nada to trick me into going up there after him and then was waiting for us when we busted into the casa."

"He is a rich man's son. I know him, now that I think about the little cocksucker," Don Carlos said. "Actually a spoiled child."

"Where does his money come from?" Angela asked.

"Mexico City. His father has much money."

"Enough to pay for all those guards?" Slocum asked.

"That would be nothing to him." Don Carlos made a pained face when he shifted in the chair. "By the way, I have asked Donna to marry me. I hope you're happy."

"Did she say yes?" Slocum asked and then smiled.

"I think so," Don Carlos said and then laughed. "Yes, she did."

"You're lucky."

"Who is lucky?" Donna swept into the room.

"Him," Slocum pointed at Don Carlos. Everyone laughed.

Donna smiled, then said, "Slocum, I have a hot bath for you being made ready upstairs. Send your clothing right down and wear the largest robe I have set out for you until they dry."

"Yes, ma'am." He winked at Angela. "Here's to Angela." He raised his glass high. "For getting us out of that damn prison."

Everyone agreed.

Slocum and Angela went upstairs. When he opened the door, he spotted the steaming tub. "Whew, she aims to cook me."

Angela poked him. "That place was pretty bad."

"Yeah, I can still smell it."

After his bath he busied himself shaving. "So whatever brought you back?"

"Oh, I knew you were in trouble. My dreams were all about you. You kept me awake. I worried the ones holding you might kill you before I could get up here. I found Cherrycow here in the village earlier. He took me to Don Carlos's, and from there I went to work."

"I owe you my life." He swished the soap and whiskers off the blade in the pan of hot water, then went back to slicing off his stubble.

"Maybe I owe you more than that. Don't worry about it."

"What about your rancher deal?" Slocum frowned for an answer.

When he glanced at her for a reply, she stared at the ceiling for help. "Oh, he has so many problems, no wonder he has no woman. What I suspected about him, it happened. And oh, he is such a poor lover, my God, there was no way I could live with him."

"Sorry." He went back to shaving. "I still don't have Martina McCarty away from those bastards. In fact I haven't found her. Can you help me?"

"I will look for her."

"Good, I can damn sure use the help. Salazar says he has her son too."

"You said—"

"I know the pistoleros were angry over him saying that. Why would that bastard say that if he didn't have the boy?"

She stretched her arms over her head. "Hombre, I have no idea. The rest will be taking siestas since they were up all night. Can we?"

He laughed, rinsing off his face with a wet cloth. "It ain't sleep you want."

She shrugged. "Oh, we can do that later."

Then she ripped off the towel from around his waist and moved in to hug him. "You know what I need."

Yes, he knew all right.

13

Much, much later, after a splendid supper fixed by Donna's crew that evening, they discussed the issue of Salazar and Martina McCarty.

"Maybe he has sent her to Mexico City?" Don Carlos said.

"No," Slocum said. "I don't think he's done that. It sounded to me like he was having a big, hot affair with her. If he was, he wouldn't want to be separated from her. Though maybe he was just bragging or trying to make me upset." He shook his head to try to clear his thoughts.

"Oh, Señora Stallings sent you her regards, Slocum," Donna said, standing over Don Carlos. "And you need to get some sleep," she said to Don Carlos.

"Ah." Don Carlos stood. "Not even my wife yet, and already she is bossing me around." But he didn't argue any more, and she asked everyone to excuse them.

When the room was down to Slocum, his three men and Angela, they went over everything that had happened here in Sierra Vista—piece by piece. How Salazar had killed or had others kill Nada to get Slocum to try to take the casa, and then had captured him and Obregón and Jesús.

123

"And he expected that prison to hold us," Obregón said, leaning back in his chair, puffing on a great cigar courtesy of Don Carlos's generosity.

"How will we find out where she is?" Jesús asked.

"Find out if this Salazar goes anyplace besides that casa."

"That could be dangerous."

"Yes, Jesús, they know us too well. But there are men in this village who will work cheaply enough and who we can count on to get us that information. I'll give you some money, and the three of you find and hire some of them."

"How much should we pay them?"

"Oh, I'd say a dollar a day."

Obregón quickly agreed about the money. "With as little work as there is to be found up here, you could buy their life for that much."

Slocum gave them ten silver dollars. "Be extremely careful. I don't need you hombres back in that fortress's hoosegow, or in the village one."

"We don't want to go there either." Jesús laughed as they left.

Slocum rose and stretched. Maybe the morning would bring them some news. He and Angela went down the hall to the bedroom.

"Hiring those men is a good idea. I was afraid you were going to try to follow Salazar yourself," she said under her breath. "That could be the death of you."

"Well, thanks, fortune-teller. I really want Martina away from all of this. There's something fishy about this whole deal. Salazar must have her drugged up or something. She's not a whore by any means—"

He opened the door and showed Angela in. "And I missed being in bed with you." He pulled the door shut, then swung her around to kiss her. She stood on her toes, and their mouths fed on each other as he hugged her supple body and hard tits tight against him.

"Wasn't I here with you a short while ago?" she asked as he took the blouse off over her head.

"My, my," he said, admiring her firm, pointed breasts. "Was it that long ago?"

She ran her hand over the hump in the front of his pants. "Oh," she teased. "The big one must have forgotten too."

He toed off his boots. She shed her skirt, and he smiled at the sight of her shapely brown hips. It was good to have her back. He was pleased that the damn rancher couldn't hold in his cum—of course, if a man wasn't used to pussy like Angela's, he could very easily get too excited.

She shoved down his pants and stuck his root between her legs, then backed toward the bed. Tugging him along, she spread her legs into a V in the air, and he crammed his erection inside her—damn, she was a wonderful machine. Her contractions threatened to pull the cap off his dick; it was no wonder that little bastard couldn't hold on—Slocum barely could himself. Then from his aching balls he fired a round into her cavern that made her smile.

"Ah, yes, hombre. Whew!"

Intertwined, they went to sleep. He woke before dawn and eased away from her, making sure she had a light bedcover against the night's mountain coolness.

In the kitchen, he found the bride-to-be, Donna, overseeing things. He hugged her neck and then went for some fresh coffee. "Are you happy that Don Carlos finally asked you to marry him?"

"I won't have to lie to the priest at confession anymore, will I?"

"No."

She wrinkled her nose, suppressing a grin. "But I can't occasionally sleep with some horny guy like you who drops in with a *grande* dick either, can I?"

"Oh." He looked around. "You have to do it more discreetly."

She laughed and kissed him. "I'm not his yet."

Someone with a horse entered the courtyard. Slocum could hear the animal's hooves striking the stones. Gun in hand, he rushed out onto the balcony to see who it was. The rider took a wild shot at him, but his horse's jumping around spoiled his aim. The bullet smacked into the plaster. Slocum, gun ready, took aim at the rider's back. His accurate shot made the pistolero pitch forward out of the saddle, and Slocum rushed down the stairs to try to catch the wildly sidestepping horse. He didn't want the animal rushing home and telling everyone something happened to this shooter.

The horse captured, he looked up in the Chinese lantern light. All his men were out on the second floor balcony, armed, including Don Carlos.

"Who is it?" Obregón asked.

"I doubt I know him." Slocum led the animal toward the hitch rack.

"We are coming," Obregón said.

With the upset horse hitched at the rack, Slocum, gun in hand, walked over to check on the facedown hombre. When he rolled him over, the man pointed the six-gun in his hand at Slocum, who instantly kicked it away. The wounded man fell back, swearing at him.

"Who sent you?"

"Fuck you."

"Listen, if you treasure your ears, balls and dick, your tongue better move to telling me who sent you."

"You can kill me or he can—what difference does it make?"

"I can get you out of the Madres and save your ass if you help me. Otherwise I'll send word to them that you squawked on them."

The man made a pained face.

He'd hit a soft point in this bastard's armor. Now he needed to press it harder. "Who is this Cockroach?"

"That—I don't know—"

"Where does Mendez Salazar fit into this?"

"He—he is the main—one."

"Where does he hold Martina McCarty?"

"At—a small ranchero on the Río Verde. They call it the Hernandez Ranch."

"Why there?"

The man shrugged, in obvious pain from the bullet in his back.

"If I find her, you will live. If I don't, then you can expect"—Slocum made a grim face at the man—"to have your throat cut."

"She is there."

Angela was at his elbow. "You know where that ranch is?"

Slocum nodded. "I have been in that area before. It is a distance from here, but we can find it."

"When do we go?" she asked.

"As soon as we can saddle some horses. Find us some dry food." Angela nodded and went back into the house, and Slocum turned to his henchmen. "Obregón, saddle some horses and put whatever explosives we have left on a packhorse."

"Sí." The man left on the run.

Slocum turned to the other pistolero. "Jesús, I'm leaving you to guard this man. He tries to escape, kill him. And hold him until I return with Martina. If I don't come back or if I come back without her, you will end this hombre's life."

"He will need a doctor?" Jesús asked.

"Sí, but no one should speak about him."

"I savvy. He will be here waiting to be dead or alive when you return."

"Cherrycow around?" Slocum spun on his heel. No sign of him.

"We will send him to join you," Jesús said.

"Good, I may need his skills." He saw Donna coming with Angela. They carried several cloth sacks bulging with food. He hurried over and took one sack from each of them, then headed for the stables. Obregón had a packhorse ready for them, and he began stowing the supplies in the pannier. The two women worked on the other side, placing the items in that holder.

Then everything was quickly under a canvas cover and the diamond hitch was thrown on it and drawn tight. Angela ran back inside for a few personal things. Obregón led the saddle and pack animals out into the rising sunlight of the courtyard. In minutes, the three were riding out of the gate before they drew any more attention. Jesús promised to send the Apache after them.

With the way Salazar seemed to know everything, Slocum was sure that someone would report their departure to the bandit leaders, but they had to beat all the rest to the ranchero on the Río Verde. His only hope was that they beat the bandits to this remote ranch and recovered Martina first. He knew that even if she had been there, it was possible they had moved her again, unless—and this was the thing he had to hope for—they were so confident they had her well hidden that they didn't hustle her away again.

Spurring the bald-faced horse, he lead the way down alleys and backstreets, avoiding panicked loose goats and scratching chickens sent to flight at the last minute. Their iron shoes clacked on the hard rocks and street surfaces until they were at last in the pines and headed west beyond the waking town. Slocum's chest filled with anxiety. He neck-reined the good horse around obstacles of woodcutters and their burro strings on the narrow road heading back toward the village.

His resolve to find his friend's hostage wife was steeled in his thinking and goals. Anyone or anything in his way he planned to mow down. It had been long enough. Enough time had been wasted—Nada had paid with her life. Slocum was worked up enough to finish this rescue and bring his enemies to some kind of justice fast.

By nightfall, the three had gone over the high pass above the tree line and started off down the western slope. Under the stars, he had slowed their speed to a careful crawl, and when they reached a spring in the timber, he shut them down. They strung a picket rope, left the animals saddled and fed them some grain in nose bags while their riders gnawed on some jerky and slept a few hours, wrapped in individual blankets that barely kept away the nighttime coolness at the high altitude.

Stiff and sore, Slocum woke as the distant dawn began to

lighten the sky. He shook his two posse members from their sleep, and they rolled up their blankets like numb puppets and resumed the chase.

Strange that Salazar had moved Martina to the western slopes. Who would have suspected such a switch? He would have thought Salazar would have taken her to Mexico City. Maybe all this time he had underestimated Salazar and needed to reconsider his assessment and start thinking of him as more than a simple, spoiled rich man's son. If he was the Cockroach, how had he convinced all these men to ride for him and be loyal while he lulled around in the background?

Descending the mountains in the lead, Slocum wondered more and more about the man. What didn't Slocum know about him? Lots, if Martina had fallen in love with him. Nada had only been looking for information, and that had gotten her killed. She had been his bait. The worst part was, she'd been doing it for Slocum's sake; at the dance, he'd asked her to learn what she could from Mendez. But there were no answers to all his questions—how did the man hold these bandits in such a strong fashion? Be damn interesting to know.

All day long they rode through the twisting canyons on little-used trails that coursed the ponderosa pines. In late afternoon, the way brought them to the Río Verde, a cool, clear trout stream that wandered off the mountains in places, creating some high falls in the upper reaches and rushing across long meadows in others. By the early evening, they were close enough to the ranch headquarters by Slocum's reckoning. He drew up not only to rest the animals but to scout the set of buildings down the valley. He regretted that Cherrycow had not caught up with them by this time. Instead he sent Obregón to scout the ranch coming in from the west.

Belly down next to a stream with his hat off and his face submerged in the cold water, Slocum cooled the skin on his cheeks that the reflective sun had baked all day. The liquid restored some of the moisture the sun had wrenched out of his tight skin. Rising up from the ground, he shook his face to get the water clear, then he listened. Someone was coming off the mountain above them. The click of iron shoes on the faraway rocks was distinct.

"Company?" Angela asked, sitting on her butt, barefoot and checking her toenails.

He nodded, then went over and unsheathed his .44-40 from its scabbard. Then he squatted down beside her. "I sure hope that's the Apache."

"I understand. If it's not, we don't need to go to shooting, do we?"

"Not if quiet force can take him."

"He's waving. It must be Cherrycow."

"Good. Just in time." He went and put his rifle up.

After the men exchanged handshakes, Angela fed them some jerky. Obregón came back to camp with little information about who was down there at the ranch. He looked grateful to see his cohort. They all sat around in the cool afternoon waiting for the sun to set. Cherrycow said the man that Slocum had shot at Don Carlos's casa might die. But it was no great loss to them.

Night fell, and they waited until all the lights were out before they slipped off the hill, headed for the ranch. He sent the Apache ahead because he was the quietest. They met Cherrycow behind the corral and squatted down so as not to be noticed.

"There are three men here. They must not expect any trouble. They are drunk, and I can't tell if Señora McCarty is in the main casa."

"You two take out the guards. Angela and I will check out the main house. If she's here, we may need another horse for her to ride."

Obregón nodded. "We can find one."

"Good. Let's go then," Slocum said. With Angela behind him, he eased his way to the larger adobe structure that shone in the starlight. On the porch, he tried the front door, but it must have been barred inside. He slipped around the side and pried open a hinged window. Listening in the night, other than the crickets, he could hear nothing. He made a motion for Angela to stay outside. Once he was inside the empty room, his gritty soles on the tile floor made enough noise that he feared waking up the Mexican army. He moved down the hallway to a bedroom in the back of the house.

Starlight shone on a bed, and a woman slept on her side in the shaft of light coming in through the window. He recognized Martina—no one else appeared to be in the house.

He went to the bed. "Wake up, Martina. We must leave here."

"Huh? Is that you, Mendez?" Her voice was slurred; she sounded drunk.

"No, I'm Slocum. Your husband sent me to take you home."

"No!"

"Martina, your husband needs you."

She rubbed her sleepy eyes with her palms; the low-cut, silky nightgown exposed her proud cleavage as she sat up.

"I can't go with you. They will kill my son, Reginald." She began to cry. "That is why I cannot leave here." Her voice caught on a sob. "You don't understand, he has my son."

"No, he's lied to you. Your son is at the hacienda with your husband. Salazar's lied to you. Now get dressed."

"No! No! I know they have him. They will kill him if I leave here."

"They can't kill him. They don't have him." He grasped her by the arm. "Now get dressed or I'll take you out of here in that nightgown."

"No! No! He will kill him." She flailed her fists at him.

"I'll get her dressed. Go get the horses," Angela said, who had slipped inside while Slocum was arguing with Martina. "I think the others have taken care of the guards."

When Slocum opened the front door and went outside, he could still hear Martina's protests in the back bedroom. What possessed her so? Her son had been at the ranch the whole time. What did she mean—*kill him*? How did Salazar get such control over people? Whole armies of outlaws did his thievery. Like the reason for the attack on the McCarty Hacienda, there were so many questions unanswered.

"The guards chose to fight us," Obregón said. "They are dead."

With a grim set to his mouth, Slocum nodded. "We may have to tie the señora up. She thinks that they have her son and will kill him if she leaves with us."

Obregón shook his head. "Has she lost her mind?"

"I know she was a very levelheaded woman before, but now the devil possesses her. This man Salazar is a brain twister."

"What shall we do?"

"Don't let her run off. Keep a close eye on her until we safely get her home."

"I will warn Cherrycow."

"Do that." Slocum bridled a gentle horse he found in the corral and then saddled him. He led the mount to the yard gate and hitched it there. Wondering how Angela was getting along, he dreaded the notion that he might have to rope and tie Martina.

He found Angela pushing Martina, "dressed" for the most part, out of the house. Her eyes red from crying, she still tried to balk as Angela moved her none too gently to where Slocum had hitched the horse.

"Promise me that you won't run and I won't tie you on this horse," Slocum said quietly to Martina.

Her pleading face tightened. "You don't understand. They have Reg, and you are signing his death warrant by taking me away from here." She dropped to her knees in protest, crying.

No way. He hoisted her up roughly and then put her on the horse, tying her wrists to the saddle horn. Ignoring her loud protests, he put a lead on her mount and handed the rope to Angela. "You lead her."

"Oh, thanks," Angela said, mounting the horse Cherrycow brought her. "Where do we go now?"

"First to Don Carlos's house, then on to the McCarty Hacienda." Hc swung on board the bald-faced horse and waved for them to follow him. Looking at Martina's wet face made his stomach roil as though snakes were inside. *I am bringing her home—but not the way you might think, amigo.*

14

After two days of hard riding, they slipped into Don Carlos's courtyard under the cover of night.

"Ah, you have found her." The *patrón*, looking recovered, grinned down at them from the second story balcony in the Chinese lantern light.

Slocum nodded and stepped over to untie the restraints at the saddle horn that he had kept on Martina's wrists. Then he plucked Martina out of the saddle. No telling how much weight she had lost—she hadn't been eating, and that was going to kill her.

"Take care of her," he said to Angela.

Angela swept back a stubborn wave of hair from her face. "Is there a cell here to hold her?"

Donna, who had just come out of the house, looked shocked at Angela's question. "Why?"

"She is under the spell of a vicious man and will return to him if she gets the chance. She can't help herself."

"Isn't that the McCarty woman?"

Angela nodded. "But she isn't in her own mind."

"Oh, help me," Martina begged and desperately grasped for Donna. "They will kill my son. They won't listen."

"I'm so sorry," Donna said, then spoke to Angela. "Come with me."

Slocum and Angela followed and, after more struggles and wailing, McCarty's upset wife was soon locked in a secure bedroom from which she couldn't escape. Angela collapsed against the hall outside the room. Slocum came by and squeezed her shoulders.

"Thanks, Donna," he said and led his worn-out companion away to the kitchen for some food.

"Won't she need to eat?" Donna asked, following them as they went down the hallway.

Angela shook her head. "I couldn't get her to eat a thing."

"I'll try later," Donna said. "Oh, you missed the *federales*. They were here again looking for you, Slocum."

"Great, what did they want?" he asked.

"They never said. But Captain Peralta spoke with Don Carlos. Maybe he will tell you what they discussed." Donna appeared to be in a huff.

Slocum smiled. "I'll ask him."

The crew was busy eating hot food when they entered the kitchen. A young woman handed both Slocum and Angela plates loaded with food. Someone poured them wine in crystal glasses and made a place for the two of them at the long preparation table. Don Carlos was talking to Slocum's men, and Jesús joined them, acting grateful to see them.

"How is the wounded man?" Slocum asked.

"He will live," Jesús said. Then he started quizzing Obregón about the rescue.

Obregón warned Jesús with a hard look on his face. "The señora is not the same. They have drugged her or twisted her brain."

Upon hearing the news, Jesús looked as upset as the other two were by this turn of events. "Slocum," he raised his voice. "Slocum, who can cure her?"

"We don't know the source of the control over her. Angela knows much about such things. But after two days with her, she doesn't understand what is making Martina so convinced they have her son and will kill him for letting us take her away. We know the boy is with poor Mitch at the hacienda, waiting for his mother's return."

"Why did Salazar have her in such an isolated place?" Don Carlos asked.

Slocum shrugged. "Maybe to trap us. But we beat him at his own game."

"You would think any poison that he fed her would have worn off by now," Don Carlos said.

"No," Angela said. "He has a power. It is not medicine. This is embedded in her head."

Food platters were passed around the table. Some took second helpings, and they went back to eating.

"Slocum, what will you do next?" Don Carlos asked.

"Take Martina home to be with her son and maybe she will believe the truth."

"And then?"

"Then—I owe Salazar my full attention. He obviously murdered Nada and no doubt is a big part of this Cockroach deal."

"You know his father is very influential in Mexico City."

"I've heard that. Is that why the *federales* came here?" Slocum asked.

"I talked to Captain Peralta. The father thinks authorities in the *Norte* are picking on his heir."

"What does Peralta think?"

"He is unsure. I told him this Cockroach business has been causing widespread crime over the region, and he agreed, but he has no idea about the source of it either."

"Maybe we can convince him who it centers on."

Don Carlos shook his head wearily. "He is dead set that Salazar is not involved."

"Then he has to be taught some facts."

"Be careful. He considers you a foreign troublemaker."

"Good." Slocum forced a laugh. "He will be a big help in solving this whole operation, I can tell already."

* * *

They left before sunup, took the backstreets and hoped they could descend the eastern slopes undiscovered in a swift flight. The distraught Martina's hands were again tied to her saddle horn and the woman looked like a rag doll in the saddle. Her situation made Slocum sick. Even Donna had not gotten her to eat anything substantial. Maybe she ate enough to keep herself alive, but that was all.

Cherrycow and Obregón made a scouting run ahead of them to look for any ambush planned to stop them. Slocum knew he would have to replace a few horses that were getting weak under the push. Maybe he could find some stout horses along the way. He still had enough money in his pocket from McCarty that he should be able to afford some new mounts. He could not believe that the outlaws had not searched him for his wealth when they shoved him into that prison. Oh well, that one thing had gone right anyway. So early during the second day on their way out of the Madres, Slocum asked Obregón to push ahead and look for the horses they needed.

At a small village, Obregón and two vaqueros waited for their arrival. The six horses they had brought for Slocum's inspection looked sound, tied at the church hitch rail.

"Angela, look them over. You need a fresh horse," Slocum said, swinging off his own horse.

She agreed with a nod, stepped down and handed her reins to Jesús, who rode in to assist her. He then quickly dismounted and undid her girths. She ran her hand over the neck of one of the horses and asked Obregón if he thought the deep red sorrel would do. The pistolero agreed with a nod and they untied him.

Slocum cradled his rifle in his arms and told Jesús that when he had Angela's saddle on, he should replace his own mount and the dun pack animal that was favoring its right hoof. Obregón nodded that he'd heard and took another horse from the rack for the dun's substitution.

"He's a nice animal," Angela said when Slocum rode by her to pay the two vaqueros for the animals.

"A good one, I'm sure." He noticed the weariness in her

eyes. "We ever get to the hacienda, we'll take a rest."

She winked. "I doubt it."

He shook his head at her disbelief and dropped to the ground. Sliding the Winchester into the scabbard, he nodded at the two traders.

"They are good horses. Thank you. What is the price Obregón negotiated with you?"

"Thirty-five dollars a head," the older man said. "And the ones that you are trading."

"You know these were good horses and can recover."

"*Sí*, señor, and our horses are fresh and sound."

Slocum counted out the purchase price, and the man politely thanked him with the money in his palm.

"If you ever need more good horses, come see me, señor." The man nodded to him.

"I'll do that. Let's ride," he called out loudly enough for the others to hear him. His concerns increased that they were staying too long in one place and made him feel it was urgent that they move on. In the saddle, he left in a trot for the east. In three, maybe four days they would be at the hacienda—without any resistance, he hoped.

He felt better when, two days later, they reached the Strycker place. Hans frowned at the sight of Martina and shook his head at Slocum. "What have they done to her?"

"They stole her mind."

"Is there nothing you can do for her?"

"No, and she refuses to eat as well. She says they have her son, which we know is not true, and they've convinced her that they will kill him for her leaving with us."

The man narrowed his eyes. "This is La Cucaracha business, no?"

"There is no Cockroach. I think a man called Mendez Salazar is behind it all."

"I have heard of him. His father is very rich. Why is he heading this?"

"He's a spoiled brat. Loves power and has some way to bend people's minds. Like he did to Martina."

"What is the federal government doing?"

"Sending out troops to arrest people like me who have stood up to them."

Hans nodded. "I understand."

"I need to go check on my people." Slocum shook the man's hand and headed for the place where his group had dismounted.

He drew Obregón aside. "You are to watch Señora McCarty. Angela needs a good night's sleep. I know you are upset as I am about her condition, but we need to give Angela some relief."

"I savvy. But she gets no better?" The concern over Martina's condition showed in his dark eyes.

"No better."

"What will the *patrón* do?"

"I have no idea, but he too will be worried at her mental state." He headed for Angela and drew her back from her ward. "Obregón will watch her tonight. You need some sleep."

Numbly she agreed. "I don't know if she has the strength left to even sit a horse."

"In a couple of days, we'll have her home, but her condition will hurt Mitch more than the loss of his arm."

Angela leaned on him. "Oh, yes, even more so."

"Come on. Let's find some privacy." He carried his bedroll on his shoulder, and they went out in the chaparral to be by themselves. To clear the space, he kicked away the rocks and then spread the bed out on the ground. They both quickly undressed and then fell into each other's arms. The duration of their connection was short but tender. Then both fell sound asleep.

Slocum was up before the sunlight even threatened the distant horizon. Quickly he dressed, the cold air sweeping his bare skin and stealing the warmth from their bond under the covers. He left Angela to sleep and went to check on things. Obregón was asleep with his back to the building where Martina slept. He awoke at Slocum's footfall.

"Ah, amigo, I was only resting my eyes." Then the pistolero laughed softly.

Slocum squatted on his haunches beside his man and agreed. "The nights get shorter and shorter. She inside?"

"Yes, there is no way to escape but get by me."

"Weak as she is, there is little chance she dug herself out?" Slocum asked, considering the chance.

"No, she couldn't do that. What can they do for her?"

"I hope seeing her son safe will finally restore some of her sanity."

Obregón crossed himself. "Mother of God, I hope so. Sometimes such things are worse than death."

"I agree. We better get the others up and prepare something to sustain us. It is still a long ride to the hacienda. But I want to get there quickly."

"*Sí*, my wife and family must wonder where I have been."

"Hell and back."

"Ah, *sí*, there too."

Angela soon joined them, and the men built a fire for her to cook on. By the orange light reflecting on her face, Slocum decided she looked more rested. There were some strips of fresh beef that their host sent down for her to cook and some onions she diced to cook with it. Slocum thanked the young woman who delivered the meat, and she nodded before running back in the emerging first light.

The men were anxious to have something fresh and teased Angela as she prepared their meal. Obregón brought Martina down to the fire, where she sat on the ground, still alone in her own depressed world.

Martina looked tired and worn out. If only she would eat. Slocum had no answer for that matter. She might not be alive in many more days at this rate. But he knew of no way to raise her spirits either—perhaps seeing that her son was safe and that her husband needed her would be the spark to kindle a fire inside her. He was ready to kick her butt, but knew that would not do anything. This whole business had been so defeating—from the start. The spell the *bruja* in San Antonio had put on him—but Angela had thwarted her spell. Still, Martina was even worse off than he had been—only a powerful wizard could ever bring her out of it, unless the sight of her family became a new dawn in her life. He could only hope for that to happen.

They took to the road before sunup and were drawing closer every hour. When night fell, Slocum thought it was better to push on, since they were close to their destination.

At last, their horses hanging their weary heads down, they coughed in the dust as they plodded up the main road of floury dirt to the McCarty Hacienda. The stars even looked dull in the great black sky. But the beacon of the few lights on at the hacienda was enough to force Slocum at least to be grateful. If they had to go another kilometer, the horses would no doubt have balked on them or tumbled nose down into the loose dirt in complete exhaustion.

"I can see it," Angela said in a hoarse voice.

"We'll be there in a short while," he promised her. Then, seeing that Martina was on the verge of fainting, he spurred his horse in close and swept her out of the saddle.

She didn't even respond.

"Don't die on me now!"

15

Mitch's booming voice shattered Slocum's sleep. "Mi amigo! Yeah, you made it back—barely, huh?"

Dull headed, Slocum sat up in the great feather bed and blinked in the bright sunlight streaming in the windows when the one-armed man swept the tall red drapes back from the panes.

"Is she . . . ?" Dread stabbed deep in his heart. Was Martina alive? His memory of sweeping her off her horse and feeling her body limp in his arms, followed by the welcome of the night before, was all blending together in a haze that he could not separate out enough to recall.

"Sleeping. But she ate something last night."

"Good." He lay back down and stared at the peeled ceiling timbers that supported the tall roof. "I'm sorry. We did our best."

"More than most would do. Get up. They bring you bath water, a razor and towels. We plan a great fiesta for you and your army's success. No one else could have done this job so well, mi amigo."

"Has she seen that her son was well?"

"Obregón told me about that. Yes, last night, even before she ate. I think that was what helped her the most."

"I wondered—I thought it might."

"Ah, she will be fine in time, I am certain."

Slocum closed his eyes. *Thank God.*

"How can I repay you?"

"With fresh horses and supplies. I want this Salazar skinned alive."

"Whoa! Whoa! Give yourself a few days to rest up some, have some fun and dance."

"Where is Angela?"

"Bathing and getting dressed for tonight's event. That is why I came to wake you."

"Thank you. And the men?"

"At home resting—they were very impressed with what you did. They told me many things."

Slocum nodded his head in agreement. "They're loyal, tough hombres. They were a big help to me."

A brigade of pretty women carrying buckets of water burst into the room and began filling the tub and laughing. They teased Slocum about sleeping all day and promised him much food and drink if he came to the kitchen.

While they filed out, laughing at him, Mitch clapped him on the shoulder. "We are all so grateful."

Still in a daze, Slocum thanked his friend, and then Mitch took his leave. Slocum found the hot water relaxing to his stiff muscles, and he tried to go over in his head all the things that had happened since he last slept in the fine bed. Lots.

The party that evening was fun. Angela joined him, outfitted in an expensive silk dress. "Nothing is too good for any of us," she whispered behind her hand to him.

"I haven't seen Martina," he said back.

"She is better, but perhaps not ready for all this commotion."

He agreed and moved through the hustle of the invited guests, stopped by several who asked, "Aren't you the man who brought Señora McCarty back safely?"

Slocum nodded, feeling uncomfortable. He'd brought her

back all right, but perhaps broken. Certainly not "safe." She might never be her old self—the smiling, beautiful hostess of the hacienda.

"What concerns you?" Angela looped an arm through one of Slocum's and leaned against him.

"The fact that La Cucaracha is still free and no doubt up to more trouble against innocent people."

"But you are only one man. What can you do?"

"I'm working on that."

"Come with me. This is the event of my life." She snatched two glasses of champagne off the tray a server carried and handed one to him. "Let's have fun tonight. We can chase down the Cockroach later."

He saw the pleading in her sexy brown eyes. Unable to deny her this special evening, he toasted her with his glass. "To the *bruja* from the small village. May the night sparkle."

"*Gracias*, mi amigo. Don't look now, but my suitor is coming."

"Will he ask you to dance?"

"I suspect so."

"Then dance with him. It will be his thrill."

"I guess so."

The well-dressed rancher, Don Juarta, bowed and politely asked Slocum's permission to dance with Angela. Slocum restrained his amusement and solemnly said, "Certainly."

He watched them go through the crowd and just about laughed at the look of excitement on the poor man's face over having Angela in his arms. Slocum mused about her story of how extreme Don Juarta's arousal was the last time that he emptied his charge on her belly.

"I take it you are Slocum?" a tall man with a clipped mustache asked.

"Yes, but I don't think we have met." Slocum studied the man, who was tall for a Latino, maybe five-ten. He bore the stiff back of a cavalry officer. Something about him made him look important, but his dark, inquiring gaze that sized Slocum up made Slocum anxious about the man's purpose.

"What can I do for you?"

"Tell me all you know about Mendez Salazar."

"Why? He had Mitch's wife kidnapped. What else?"

"Why would an heir to a fortune in Mexico City be involved in such a common crime?"

"I guess because it's a thrill."

The man gave a short, silent nod as if factoring Slocum's words into some theory he held. "Will that be the end of his law breaking?"

"No. He's involved in crimes all over the area."

"Oh, dear God, man. Can you prove it?"

"I never caught your name," Slocum said.

"Raul Donovan. My father was Irish and killed in the Mexican War with your country."

"You have taken up the sword?" Slocum asked.

"I was in the army. The military is a place to gain some rank in this country, especially with an Irish name."

"I see. And today?"

"Today I am a private citizen."

Slocum nodded. "Very good."

"Will you go and look again for this Salazar?"

"I don't think so," Slocum lied. Why had this man come to ask him all these questions? He had a purpose—good or bad. Slocum was not certain what the ex-soldier was up to, but something about the man made Slocum hesitate to trust him.

The money of Salazar's family could afford any spy they wanted to hire. This man might be such an agent for them. His father had already had the government send in the *federales* to stop any opposition—why wouldn't they hire such a slick-talking hombre as Donovan? Money meant nothing to them.

Angela was back, smiling at this man.

"Raul Donovan," Slocum said.

"Angela," she said.

"My pleasure, señora."

"*Gracias*. Excuse us, señor." Then she turned to Slocum. "I must tell you something if you are through here."

"Certainly. We must talk some more later," he said to the man.

The man agreed and then walked off with a "Later."

Slocum turned and led her to the side. "You know that hombre?"

She frowned, looking back to be certain Donovan was not in hearing. "No, but Don Juarta told me he is a member of the *presidente*'s police. And to watch him."

"I figured as much. No doubt he is being financed by Salazar's father."

"What shall we do?"

"Silence all the talk of our going back out to find Salazar."

"How do you do that?"

"Tell Francisco to keep our preparations secret and have the ranch help to do the same. I'll do this later tonight. Donovan gets too damn nosy, we'll cut off his nose."

She laughed and then covered her mouth as if embarrassed.

He hugged her shoulder. "Two of us can surely outmaneuver him."

"I hope so."

Later Slocum found the McCarty's *segundo* and told him the problem.

Serious-faced, Francisco asked, "You want me to have him killed?"

Slocum shook his head to dismiss his concern. "I can handle him."

"I will be sure nothing is said about the preparations."

"Gracias." Slocum returned through the kitchen and smiled at the busy crew before reentering the party. Angela soon found him, and he explained his absence. She nodded in agreement.

Slocum knew that McCarty had earlier excused his wife Martina from the festivities because she tired easily. Slocum had only seen her at a distance. Behind her smile she still wore a haggard appearance. His only contact with her since they returned had been brief, and she'd thanked him. But while she had obviously made some improvement, she was a long way from being herself. She might never fully recover.

Angela made Slocum dance to the band of musicians, and he swung her around the floor. Out of breath, they moved to the edge of the crowd.

"You probably dance much better in a cantina." She laughed and then threw her hair back from her face, smoothing it down.

"Ah, yes, but you are enjoying this so much, maybe you should reconsider a life with Juarta."

"You tease me, of course. I can find better men than him, or I'd go back and be happy living in that jacal where you found me."

He swept her up and kissed her.

"Who—" she said, coming from his embrace. Then she stopped. "Who is that man talking with Donovan now?"

"I never saw him before. Have you?"

"*Sí*, in the village in the mountains. I saw him in the square, when I was searching for you."

"Donovan must have more spies here."

"What will they try next?"

"I don't know, but I would say they are concerned about me going back up there."

She agreed. "I will go dance with Juarta. He may know the man's name."

"Be careful. I'll watch for him."

"Don't worry, they won't catch me sleeping."

Slocum spotted a cattle buyer who shipped cattle up to the United States from the border and paused to speak to him. "How is business?"

"So-so. One day it is good, next day no one wants them. Like the old rail markets dried up on us. Cattle shipping costs are too high to ship and then sell them. We were better off taking a dozen boys and driving them to Kansas. But there are so many barbwire fences it's nearly impossible to drive them overland now."

Slocum agreed, and they shook hands and parted. Then he met Angela and led her off to the side. "Did Juarta know the man?"

She shook her head. "But I saw another man from up in the mountains. His left ear was cut off at some time."

With a slow shake of his head, Slocum tried to recall an earless man. But he couldn't think of one he'd seen up there, other than the one whose ear he'd cut off himself, but this man was not him. He may have had long hair to disguise his loss. That needled him. Donovan had the party loaded with his spies, and they might be there to eliminate the pistoleros as well. In fact, it seemed very likely to Slocum that his pistoleros were in immediate danger.

"Come on," he said.

He rushed through the kitchen with Angela on his heels. "I need to find Francisco."

"He has gone to his casa," one of the sweaty-faced women said, then lifted her large, stained apron to wipe her wet face.

"Can you point it out?"

"Rachel, show him Francisco's casa," she said to a younger girl who shed her apron and led them on the run.

The casa was a good ways from the hacienda. Hurrying down the dusty road, he wondered if Angela needed to stop, she was huffing so hard. But she waved him to go on.

"Francisco!" he shouted at the dark adobe house.

A lamp flickered on in the casa. The man shouted, "Coming!"

Slocum put his hands on the plaster wall and tried to recover his wind. Angela collapsed on the ground, and the young girl who had brought them coughed, supporting herself with her hands on her knees.

"What is wrong, amigo?" Francisco asked, dressing in his shirt as he came outside.

"There are some men here at the party who I think will try or have already tried to kill your pistoleros."

"Who are they?"

"I only have one name—Donovan."

"I don't know him. Here, take a rifle."

"Thanks," Slocum said, taking the cartridges Francisco offered first and then the Winchester rifle. "There is one of them who lost his left ear. You know of anyone like that?"

Francisco made a face in the light coming from outside. "I have heard of such a man, if he is the same one."

Several mounted guards had come on horseback to see what was wrong. Their boss immediately gave them orders. "Take four men and go find Obregón, Jesús and Cherrycow. There are killers here who may try to kill them."

"*Sí*, we are on our way," one man promised, then picked three others to accompany him. The four galloped off, and the others milled around on their mounts.

"Go back to the house and keep your eyes open for anyone leaving who looks like trouble. Try to hold them, but if they show arms, kill them."

The riders left for the house.

Francisco said, "I have some horses I keep saddled out in back just in case. Will Angela come with us?"

Slocum nodded. Recovered, Angela nodded and ran with them around the casa. Slocum drew up a cinch for her and tossed her on a horse. She nodded that all was well with her and gathered the reins.

"We don't know if they left the house. Let's check there first." Slocum on his mount led the way under the stars, down the road reflecting the moon between the knee-high irrigated crops beside it.

Two house guards came out back, and their boss asked them if any men without women had left.

"A few left shortly after Señor Slocum left."

"Which direction?"

"West, when they left here."

"Did anyone know them?"

"One was Colonel Donovan. Juan said that he used to be in the army."

"What about a one-eared man?" Slocum asked.

"*Sí*, I saw him leave too after Donovan left."

"Maybe they have left the ranchero?" Francisco asked Slocum.

"We won't know until your guards return."

Francisco made a pained face in the moonlight. "Why do you think they want to kill the pistoleros?"

"Because they helped me and know much of this Cockroach deal."

"What is all the commotion about out here?" Mitch asked, coming out the kitchen door.

Slocum held his finger to his lips and lowered his own voice. "We think some assassins were here tonight and may still be on your place."

In the starlight, Mitch frowned. "On my ranch?"

"There was a man here named Donovan. A suspect who I think is the leader."

"I know that man. What has he done?"

"You better watch him. He's connected to the others I don't trust."

"What is their purpose?"

"I think to learn if I was going back after Salazar and maybe to kill the three men who helped me."

"Holy shit. How did you learn all this?"

"Angela saw a man here tonight that was in the village in the mountains, who had lost an ear."

Mitch nodded. "I saw him once and wondered who had sent him an invitation."

"La Cucaracha did, is my guess."

"Oh, damn. What about the pistoleros?"

"I sent four good men to the workers' village," Francisco said. "To be sure they were warned and safe."

"Where did the others who left the party go?" Mitch asked.

"*Patrón*, the guards here say they rode west."

Slocum had dismounted. "But they may have circled back."

"Who do these devils work for anyway?"

"Well, Mitch, I think they all work for the Cockroach. This man Donovan is smarter than his foot soldiers."

Mitch shook his head in disbelief. "Who can we trust?"

"Us." Slocum laughed and hugged Angela, who was under his wing.

16

Their naked bodies sent off sparks in the feather bed. Slocum, at last, hunched his throbbing dick through Angela's wet gates. Hard-to-catch breathing racked out of their throats as the power in his legs and hips drove his shaft deep inside her with each plunge, causing her jaw to drop open as pleasure swallowed her. His eyes half closed in satisfaction, he enjoyed the sheer forces created between them as they soared over the high road of passion.

Her butt lifted off the mattress, she thrust her hips at his swollen erection. Harder and faster, she fought to reach the mountain peak, her mouth open as she moaned with the excitement and pleasure. She at last strained against him and he came deep inside her. They collapsed in a pile, mouth feeding off mouth, snuggled together, still attached as their excitement seeped into flushed relaxation. Her arms wrapped tight around him, she smothered her firm breasts against his chest.

"Let's stay here forever." Angela threw her arms aside and snuggled her back in the soft mattress of goose down.

Braced up over her, Slocum smiled down at her sleepy eyes and the relaxed look on her face. "Nothing I'd like better."

"Whew, this has been as exciting as my honeymoon. A new dress, a great dance and a party. Such a long ways from being practically kidnapped by a man twice my age, who awed me half to death, took me to a priest he woke up to wed us and then took my virginity in a haystack and led me to this fuzzy state of pleasure in a stable. My head spun for days and nights after that—it was so wonderful then for a dumb girl from a small village. I didn't live in this world then though."

He used the side of his index finger to lift her chin and took the honey from her mouth. Licking his lips, he shook his head and asked, "What did the hay smell like?"

She laughed. "A very strong, dried grass smell, but who cared? My husband was a strong lover, almost like you, and he lasted long. I thought everyone had sex three or more times a day back then."

Then with a mischievous smile, she snickered and shook her head in obvious disbelief. "Should we dress and find breakfast—?" A knock on the door made them both frown.

Slocum reached over for his Colt and cocked it. "Yes?"

"Señor, the *patrón* asks you come at once to the great hall."

"I'm coming." He set the gun down and hopped out of bed to dress. He pulled his shirt over his head first. Then he fought the leather britches on and sat down to put on socks and yank on his high-top boots. She tied on the silk kerchief around his neck and looked him in the eye. "What is wrong?"

"I have no idea. Dress and join me."

She agreed and jumped up to struggle into her silk dress. He buttoned up the back, and she put on her slippers as they headed for the door, reaching down to pull them on. She re-set the dress's waist in the hall, then hurried to keep up with him. At last, trying to tame down her mussed hair, she entered the hall beside him. Slocum gratefully saw his three men there, with sombreros in their hands.

"What is wrong?" Slocum asked when he acknowledged them.

Mitch turned in his high backed chair. "You were right. They did try to kill my men."

"Who was it?" Slocum looked at the three pistoleros standing aside.

"We don't know his name. We call him One Ear."

Slocum narrowed his eyes to look hard at his friend. "The one at the party?"

"*Sí.*"

"Will he talk?"

Mitch shook his head. "He quit breathing."

Slocum showed Angela to a chair and took another beside his friend. "How did he die?"

"He tried to kill Cherrycow, but he probably chose the wrong one to start with. He made enough noise to awake Cherrycow, who grabbed his hunting knife and cut his throat when he climbed in his window."

"Good for him," Slocum said. "Who do you think he is?"

"I had seen him before on the border, but I don't know what they called him."

"That the only one who tried anything?" Slocum searched the others for answers.

"The arrival of the guards scared them off," Obregón said. "We know now that there were four more riders. We found their tracks, but the guards trailing them must have spooked them."

Francisco came in from the kitchen.

Mitch waved him over. "What did you learn?"

"Those riders who were at the workers' village last night, we tracked them back to here and lost them in the dust of all the others."

McCarty nodded and turned back to Slocum. "You discovered them, but how I don't know. What do I do now?"

"I believe that Salazar sent them, concerned that I was going to go back to get him. Donovan apparently didn't believe me when I said I wasn't going to pursue Salazar," Slocum said.

McCarty pounded the table. "Is there no end to these bastards?"

Slocum shook his head. "No end till we get Salazar."

"Bring these men some food," the *patrón* said over his shoulder. Someone in the doorway called back, "It is coming."

"You men sit down."

The three pistoleros looked at one another.

McCarty slapped the table. "Sit down. These chairs won't bite you."

The men moved quickly to take seats.

Soon platters of food and fruit were brought by the kitchen workers. Goblets were filled with wine, and the pistoleros nodded in approval. They began to eat, sharing quiet words. Angela sipped some fresh-squeezed orange juice, listening closely and offering some quiet words to Slocum.

He agreed with her comments. The next trip to the mountains would be fraught with ambushes to stop him. That meant they feared him—good.

After lunch, Slocum shook hands with his men and told them he'd call on them soon to go back, but not to tell anyone. "I want surprise to be on our side—of timing if nothing else—now that he knows we'll be coming for him."

"Slocum, when should we leave?" Obregón asked.

"We need to be secret, but within the next two days I think we need to go back."

"*Gracias*, we will be ready."

When they were through eating, Mitch thanked them and told them he would pray for their success. "May God help you."

The men left, wiping their greasy lips with their kerchiefs. It would be something to tell their coworkers, that they had eaten in the great hall. Like Angela, who had been so impressed with the party and her new dress, these men had touched the aristocracy of their world.

Horses were being shod by the blacksmiths. Supplies loaded into panniers. Packsaddles repaired. Quietly the hacienda worked to get the party ready to return to the Madres. Slocum cleaned his arms and oiled them. He was working at a table in the flower garden under some shade with his pistol parts spread out on newspaper. Angela had gone to take a bath in another room down the hall with two young girls helping her. Slocum looked up when someone approached his work bench.

"Slocum, I came to thank you again." Martina took a seat across the table from him.

He studied the .44's bore and, satisfied that it was clean, set it down on the paper. The woman who sat opposite him still looked tired. Her once-bright brown eyes remained dimmed.

"Martina, I hope you can find your way back."

"I am trying, but it is hard."

"I can only imagine how hard it is. Do you recall anything about Salazar that would help me?"

"It is all a blur. I can't even reconstruct it in my mind."

He nodded. "Do you recall his actions or anything when he first came back to see you each time?"

"I remember he would clap his hands, and then I don't recall much else after that. I could only recall how sore I was after I regained my mind. I could only imagine what had happened to me."

"They told you they would murder Reg if you didn't obey them?"

She nodded. "I couldn't believe anything else. I believed in my heart that they held him as a prisoner."

"This Cockroach, he's a mind twister." Slocum shook his head. "I recall a surgeon during the war who could control people's pain when he had to operate without anesthesia. I have been trying to think of what they called that—hypno . . . something. It only came to me yesterday. I was thinking all this time about spells cast by witch doctors."

"What is it?" She asked and reached over to grasp his forearm. "You mean this is the thing he used on me?"

"It froze your mind, and you did what he commanded you to do."

"That and I truly believed he held my son and that they would kill him if I left him."

"I am afraid that is what he is doing to other people."

"Where could he learn how to do such a thing?"

"Some professor in France maybe taught him this business. I recall hearing they had run the man out of England."

"Wouldn't that be very expensive?"

"His father is very rich, so it would be no problem for him. He no doubt traveled overseas and learned how to do that."

"Will I ever escape his hold?"

"I think in time it wears off, but it is timed with a hand clap, so you will need to be careful."

"I shall, and thanks. Perhaps now I can return to my family as a wife and mother and not fear that his hold on me will strengthen again."

"Slocum?" Obregón removed his sombrero and bowed his head when he joined them. "Excuse me, Señora McCarty. I came to tell Slocum something and did not realize you were here."

"What is wrong? It is all right, she will understand."

"I talked to some packers today who brought some gold out of the Sierras. They say there is a large party of bandits waiting above the Strycker Hacienda. The packers said they heard the bandits were waiting for you."

"Good." Slocum smiled. "They may wish they'd stayed home."

"Oh, be careful." Martina's look registered her alarm.

"Don't worry. I have a surprise for them." Slocum stood up and reached over to hug her head. "You will recover. Your whole life is ahead of you."

"You two and the others are very brave men. May God go with you."

"Sí," Slocum agreed. "We will need his help too."

After Martina left the garden to the two men, Slocum put his cleaned revolver back together and snapped in the cylinder. Then he spun it gently on his sleeve. Satisfied they were alone, he nodded at his man. "We will do something to them. Go find Cherrycow. I want these assassins scouted out. So we will put off leaving for another day."

"We can do that," Obregón agreed.

"Maybe we can come around behind them, where they least expect us to be."

"He and I will know in two days and be back here."

"Be careful, my amigos. Don't take any chances. I fear if I go they will get word and ambush us. This way we will have a plan, when you two find them."

"What else?"

"I have to ask Martina one more question."

"What is that?"

"I'll tell you when I get the answer. Talk to you later." They parted, and Slocum hurried to locate Martina inside the casa. He found her at a writing desk in an alcove, and she looked up from her correspondence.

"What is it?"

"Can you recall how many times Salazar clapped his hands to put you under?"

"I think three times . . . yes, it was three times. Why?"

"I may need it sometime if I get in a tight place."

"Hmm, that is strange."

"Why?"

"I had never really thought that was the sign that put me under his spell before we talked today."

Slocum agreed. "I'm remembering more about that doctor and how he used it on his patients."

Later, Slocum found Angela, who was sewing new britches and a long-sleeved blouse for the trip back. She and two women were cutting and sewing like mad. When she noticed that Slocum was in the room, she tried to hide her handiwork. "This was to be a surprise for you."

"Sorry to spoil your plans, but if you get surrounded by the bandits, quickly clap your hands three times."

She frowned very seriously at him. "What will that do?"

"I hope it will paralyze them. It was how he had control over Martina."

"Oh. When will we leave here?"

"We'll be here two days longer."

"Great, we will have this project completed. Two more days, girls."

"Good," the older woman said and smiled at him.

He bent over, kissed Angela's cheek and then headed out the doorway. There were many more things he needed to do. Who else at the hacienda, besides Cherrycow, could make bows and arrows to deliver blasting powder sticks? He better go find Francisco. He'd be the only one who knew that, and Slocum wanted something done along those lines.

He needed several armed and fused half sticks of blasting powder, ready to use. This was a poor man's cannon fire that would disorient the enemy. They might need several sticks ready to light and fire. This time he was going to take that damn Cockroach down and his organization with him.

17

Two days later, Slocum and his three pistoleros, along with Angela, left the hacienda under the cover of night. Three o'clock in the morning. They rode out as silent as five riders with four packhorses trailing them could. There was no moon; they would have to rely on the stars to guide them. But the desert has much more light at night than the forests of hardwood or pine in the American South where Slocum grew up. Leading the way, he felt pleased about the information his scouts had brought back. The estimated force camped beyond the Strycker Hacienda was a dozen men. Salazar had misjudged his enemy, unless these hombres were bulldogs, and Slocum doubted they were his best men. No way this hombre would expose his toughest men first. Slocum turned in the saddle to look back over his team, the acrid dust tickling his nose, and he decided everything was going fine—so far.

They stopped early the first night since they'd been riding since before dawn. In midafternoon the next day they reached the first water holes. Strycker ran outside to greet them. "Ah, señora, it is so good to see you and Slocum here. Did you have a good trip so far?"

"Oh, yes," Angela said as she dismounted. "Thank you."

"Are you and your men going back into the mountains?" Strycker looked upset about it.

Slocum nodded, then swung his chap-clad leg over the cantle and stepped down. "I don't want Salazar's men to know we are here. They're camped close by."

"I was going to tell you that they are at the crossing."

"We can handle them."

"Would you want to use some of my men?"

Slocum shook his head to stop him. "Not till dark. We must be quiet."

"Whatever you say." The man turned to Angela. "You look very well rested, my dear."

"I am fine," she said. "I bet you have some food in the house so I don't have to cook for these hombres."

"Of course, of course. Where are my manners? That was what I came out to do, invite you into my casa to feed you and the men."

"We will go around back," Obregón said. "We have the stock to put up."

"*Sí*, my men will help you," Strycker said. "You two come on inside," he said to Slocum and Angela. "I was concerned that you would walk into their trap."

Slocum shook his head. "Not very likely. Those three men with us know how to fight their way."

"They must be very brave to follow you." He turned to the older woman who ran his kitchen. "Pour them some wine and serve the food."

"*Sí, patrón*," she said and with a short bow and hurried off to get their plates.

The meal smelled delicious as the young girls served the steaming food on the table. How Strycker knew that they were coming, Slocum wasn't certain, but his plans were working out well.

The flank steak proved so tender that Slocum could cut it with a fork. The aroma of the mesquite-wood flavoring seduced him. He began wrapping some of the meat in a great flour tortilla, and his solid teeth about floated out of his gums at the mesquite-smoke flavor. There were dishes of steaming hot refried beans, black beans, rice, fried onions and sweet peppers, plus several different varieties of hot peppers. Fresh flour tortillas kept coming from the kitchen like telegrams— hot and ready.

Their wine goblets were refilled by a special servant in charge. Some musicians played classical Spanish music, and a young woman whirled across the floor, clacking castanets and her heels on the tile floor.

"I wonder where she came from," Slocum said to Angela under his breath.

She gave him a very short nod. "I think she came from the border."

"I simply wondered if she works for Salazar. You think she does?" he whispered. "She is attractive and looks healthy enough."

Angela made sure no one could hear her talking to Slocum. "Maybe."

"Really?"

She managed to say, "They can hire anyone they want."

Slocum excused himself and went to speak to his three men. He found them eating outside of the kitchen.

"Have you seen any of those bandits here tonight?" he asked them, squatting down close to where they sat on empty crates.

Obregón said, "Their camp is not so far."

Cherrycow added, "It's less than an hour's ride from here."

"Sí. No farther," Obregón agreed.

"Good. We ride at midnight. A good show of force tonight may be enough to dislodge them."

The men nodded.

"We will be ready," Obregón promised.

"Leave our supplies here. Later we can come back for them."

"Good, then we can move faster," Jesús said, sounding relieved.

The matter settled, Slocum studied the sundown bleeding in the western sky as he headed for the back door of the big house. Time for a few hours' rest. This attack would be step one in his charge to bust up La Cucaracha and his control on the mountain people.

"Strycker said we should sleep in a bed tonight." Angela met him returning.

"I guess we can trust him for a few hours' sleep."

Angela led him through the kitchen and down the side hall to the room assigned to them.

Once inside, they both scrambled in an instant into each other's arms. Her hungry mouth on his and a new whirling inside his brain took them like a tornado to the side of the bed.

In minutes they coupled on top of the bed, his swollen erection stoking her fury. Their breathing was heavy and the ache in his dick sought relief in the tight muscular confines of her womanhood—he pounded her harder.

With her mouth wide open, gasping for more breath, small moans of pleasure escaped her throat as she hunched her hips toward him for more. Passion's heat soon slicked their bellies in sweat. He thrust harder and harder until at last he felt the sharp pains of fire in his scrotum. He pressed deep and inside her tight core, ready to explode. Cold chills ran down his facial muscles as the last strength of their furious lovemaking dissolved into mild waves. He kissed her hard.

Sweeping the hair back from her blanched face, she laughed softly. "Strycker thinks we will stay here all night."

"Good. If that's what the Cockroach's spies think too, their plans won't work to get us in broad daylight on the trail."

The time for their departure began early. Slocum knew they needed an element of surprise to take the outlaws and to be certain none of them escaped to warn their leader. The men were silent as they rode west, save for the soft plod of horse hooves in the road dust and an occasional cough of a horse or his rider.

Obregón had told Slocum that a few of the outlaws up

there in the camp waiting for them were the best and toughest pistoleros that worked for any man. Cherrycow described to him how their setup was in the junipers. The bandits might be scattered about, sleeping under them to be ready, but Slocum's crew could find them by starlight.

Slocum told them to quietly collect all the bandits' horses so none could escape to warn the bandits' leader in the mountains that something was wrong. The ride under the stars went well. Far short of the bandits' camp, they dismounted and advanced on foot. Each man bore a rifle, loaded to the gate, and they spread out as they moved in.

They found the outlaws' horses hitched on a picket rope and sleeping. Quietly they led the horses off, so if any of the outlaws did escape, their mounts would not be where they left them. With the horses hidden, Slocum told Angela to stay with them until things were resolved. She agreed, and he waved his men forward.

The word passed down the line that one sleeping outlaw had been spotted. The whack of a rifle butt to the bandit's head, and there were no more sounds. Quickly their unconscious captive's arms and legs were bound and he was gagged, then they moved on. Near the smoldering fire ring, Slocum found several men asleep in peaceful rest save for some loud snoring. Each of his men, armed with a large knife, quickly silenced any protest. Several were killed immediately. The rest they hog-tied and gagged with their own kerchiefs, then sat them on the ground guarded by Jesús. The others were sought by Slocum and his other two men.

Obregón came back after a few minutes of checking around. "I think no one escaped, Slocum."

"Good."

"They were so sure of themselves they had no guards."

"What should we do with them?" Jesús asked.

"We can take their money, horses and boots, and tell them next time we see them we will kill them. Or we can shoot them when the sun comes up. Obregón, find their leader and get him out here."

"How will we decide what to do?"

"We can take a vote."

Satisfied they had all of the bandits, Obregón went among them until he had located the man in charge and dragged him by the collar back to Slocum.

"This one is the leader." Obregón removed his gag. "Tell him who you are."

"Franko, señor. We are all poor men with families. There was nothing we could do but follow his orders to ambush you. We are sorry, but these men have children and women who will be alone without them."

"What should we do with them?" Slocum asked his gathered men. Angela joined them as well.

"Just let them walk home," Obregón said.

The nod of heads around the circle of his men showed the vote.

"Mother of God, I thank you," Franko said aloud.

"Why not give them to the army as prisoners?" Angela asked quietly.

They didn't have the time, and besides, Slocum wouldn't consider such a move. "Our men have little use for them."

She agreed.

Slocum sent Jesús back to Strycker's Hacienda for the pack animals and told him to join them as quickly as possible.

They ate breakfast, left some food for their prisoners, then took the men's horses, guns and money. The outlaws had very little left but perhaps a knife and a few staples. Before the sun was above the eastern horizon, Slocum and his men trotted west for the Madres. Cherrycow and Obregón rode ahead. They took the loose horses and knew Jesús would soon rejoin them with their pack animals. The army marched on.

"By the time they walk back to the Madres, they will have thought about this deal a lot," she said.

Slocum agreed.

Midday they watered their animals at a small settlement, and Slocum bought some grain for all of them, so they had no need to stop to let the horses graze. The feeding required some time, however, because they didn't have enough nose bags for all the horses at one time. Soon they were all on their way, but not without many suspicious eyes watching them and no doubt wondering what had happened to the bandits sent to murder them.

Under way again, they pressed on for the town of Cuervo. Slocum planned to draw up short of the village, and he sent his scouts ahead after telling them his plans. While waiting for his scouts to return, he felt anxious and his belly cramped while riding along with Angela, and he began to feel deeply concerned about how his plan for the whole thing would work out.

"You didn't need any of Hans Strycker's men to back you up," she said with a head toss.

Slocum agreed. "I did not want the poor man involved later on in any revenge caused by our raid."

She agreed with a nod. "We are making good time."

"Yes," he agreed. "We can rest in the foothills where it will be cooler too."

"I understand. Don't worry about me."

"I sometimes feel guilty hauling you around on such dangerous missions."

She smiled and tossed her hair back. "I would hate to miss them."

"I understand. But this is war, and if anything happens to you, I'd be responsible."

"I simply want to be with you. Don't fret." She winked wickedly at him.

Her companionship and warmth made him feel better in the boiling dust that their horses' hooves churned up. His eyes burned watching the heat waves dazzle the distant mountains. Soon this would all be over.

18

Slocum veered to the south, taking another entry into the vast Sierra Madres. He sold the extra horses, too cheap, to a rancher who needed them. Jesús was grateful, because herding and feeding so many animals was lots of extra work for him. Slocum shared the proceeds from the sale with his men, and they rested one day in the foothills. The place they stayed was a grassy valley with a fresh stream out of the Madres to bathe in. Everyone's spirits had risen, and they were going into the mountains the next day.

Midafternoon, when all but Obregón and Cherrycow, who were scouting ahead, were taking a siesta, Slocum heard a hard-pressed horse galloping toward their camp and soon saw Obregón on his bay splashing through the stream. He grabbed his sombrero and rushed to meet him.

"What's wrong?"

"Mendez Salazar and his men are up there in the village of Los Piñones. They are drunk, raping women and children—shooting men who object."

"Why are they there?"

"Some of his men have told the villagers they planned to surprise and kill you."

166

"How did he get word we were taking this route?"

Obregón turned up his palms. "I have no idea."

Disgusted by the turn of this event, Slocum needed to know how to use this twist for their advantage. "Where is Cherrycow?"

"Scouting the place for more information."

"Salazar is with these men?"

"*Sí*, he is not hiding anymore."

"He had the same idea I had to use this trail. How many men does he have with him?"

"Hard to tell. Maybe a dozen."

"Get ready, we need to take out as many as we can to night. Drunk or pussy crazy, they will be vulnerable."

"*Sí*," Obregón agreed.

"Where is he staying? Salazar?" Slocum's mind listed his needs as he sorted out the operation ahead.

"In a large casa in the village."

"Good, this time he can't run too far."

"What is wrong?" Angela asked, hurrying over and tossing her hair from her face.

"Our man is only miles from here. Planning to come out and get us."

"So?" She searched both of their faces. "What now?"

"While they are drunk and partying tonight, we will strike and get them."

She nodded. "Good."

Half an hour later, every man was armed and ready. They rode for the village. They met Cherrycow on the road and then divided into pairs. Slocum felt his men would not be recognized in the dark and doubted many of the bandits knew them.

After sundown, they filtered into the village like a small group simply traveling through. Obregón paid a young *puta* to lure the man he thought was Salazar's captain into the alley. Once the man was outside in the dark, they conked him on the head, and then Slocum and Obregón dragged him off to a small jacal. Angela remained outside with the girl as lookouts.

"What is your name?" Slocum demanded as the man came around moaning, hands and feet tied on the cot, the candlelight bathing his angry face.

"Who—" Obregón's sharp knife blade on his jugular vein silenced him.

"Lower your voice or you won't live."

"Julio."

"Where is your *patrón*?"

"I don't—"

"You better know, 'cause your chicken neck depends on it."

"At—the casa—I guess."

"How many guards are there?"

"Four."

"How many men do you have?"

"Thirty."

"You lie. I counted the horses," Cherrycow said.

"Fifteen."

"Better." Obregón turned to Slocum. "What else do we need?"

"When did you plan to ride to kill us?" Slocum asked the man.

"Tomorrow."

Slocum considered their plans, then he nodded. Obregón made a slicing sign at his own throat. Slocum agreed. The number two man was gone. They dragged his limp body out and concealed it behind another jacal.

Angela soon joined him. "What happened?"

Slocum shook his head to indicate he'd explain later. "Tell that girl we need her to lure another one out here."

"She's scared to death."

"Better to be afraid than dead. Tell her these men have killed others in the village, but we won't let them kill her."

Angela agreed and went back to hug the girl's shoulders. The teenager must have been good at her business, for in the next hour she lured three more hired guns outside and they were eliminated. Jesús and Cherrycow soon joined them.

They had personally taken care of some of Salazar's men and gotten a couple of the real bad guys. Slocum thanked them, and then a commotion up the alley made them quiet down.

Two men were arguing over price with an older *puta*. Obregón headed in that direction, and Slocum made Angela get against the wall. A muffled gunshot sounded, and one of the bandits crumpled to the ground. The second tried to run, but one of Slocum's men clubbed him down with his gun butt. By then Slocum had the woman by the arm.

"Do you know the casa where this bandit leader hides?"

"*Sí*, señor." She was trembling.

"We are your friends. We want this bastard who leads these men."

She bobbed her head up and down rapidly. "I can show you the way."

They made the street crossing and into the next alley without drawing any notice. Several of the enemy were raising hell in the cantinas they passed. But Slocum wanted to get his hands on Salazar.

They climbed a steep hill and in the starlight, the whitewashed walls showed that the lighted grounds were well cared for. Moving beside the heavily perfumed woman, Slocum caught her arm. "Hold up. How do we get inside?"

"Go right through the kitchen. The women working in there are very upset. His men raped too many of the young girls there when they first came here."

Angela, coming on his heels, agreed with her. "We came at a good time."

Inside the kitchen, where the women were preparing for breakfast, their dark eyes looked shocked at the sight of the men, but when the *puta* put her finger to her lips, they did the same to each other.

"This man is here to take out those *bastardos*."

"Where is he?" Slocum asked.

"Top floor upstairs. There are no locks." An older women with her hands white with flour gave a head toss. "Straight ahead up there."

Pistol in hand, Slocum told Angela to stay in the kitchen, then he rushed across the great room to start up the open staircase. A man burst out of a room upstairs and fired a shot that made Slocum duck down on the steps.

Boiling, acrid gun smoke filled the two-story room, obscuring Slocum's view of the man's face, and Slocum could hear the man escaping down some back steps. Slocum changed course and ran to the rear of the house, bursting out into the starlit garden to take a shot at a running figure. But he missed. His intended victim jumped over the railing and was gone again. His boot heels clacked on the flat flagstone walk through what Slocum considered a garden—he was in hot pursuit.

If the one he followed was Salazar, he was not losing any time trying to get away. At the gate Slocum took two shots at the fleeing figure. Neither stopped him, so he must have missed again. He reloaded his Colt.

"Where did he go?" the out-of-breath Obregón asked, catching up with him.

"Down in that live oak somewhere. I must have missed him. Get the others. He'll have to come out. How did the rest do in town?"

"The bandits left are holed up in the jail. Do you want us to charge it?"

"Don't risk any of our men's lives. Blow the damn thing up."

"*Sí*. What about the man who ran off?"

"We'll get him too . . . later." He studied the live oak thicket in the ambient light of predawn. "Bring some of those blasting sticks you have left up here. We may just bring him out of there with them."

"Certainly." Then Obregón was gone.

Slocum slapped his Colt back in his holster. Angela joined him in the predawn chill, hugging her arms. "It's cold out here."

"It will soon be hot," he promised her.

"Was it him you shot at?"

"I think so. It all happened so fast, and there was not much light to shoot by."

"What will he do next?"

"Try to escape." Slocum's belly growled. They soon would need some food.

"You don't think he will try to kill you?"

"Yes, he will. Now harder than ever. Let's go back inside."

"What if he sneaks back?" She took a last look at the night and the dark live oak where the figure had disappeared.

"One thing at a time," he said and turned her toward the casa.

Obregón returned from the village while Slocum and Angela ate the fresh food prepared for them. Joining them in the kitchen, Obregón, his sombrero in hand, reported. "The jail is gone, so are the bandits. I think we got all of them. Any who are left must be burning the ground to get the hell out of there. The people of the village dragged the last two out of beds where they were raping women and hacked them to death."

"Good enough. Now we need to find Salazar. Sit down, amigo, and eat first. He can wait." Slocum indicated the seat opposite his.

"Ah, you are hungry, no?" a sweet thing from the kitchen crew asked his man and then brought him a heaping plate of food.

"Oh, gracias." Obregón looked in awe at all she brought him.

"You are very welcome, señor. You have saved all the women who work here. We are all very grateful." She curtsied for him and went back to work as the other women applauded them.

"Wow," Obregón said, sounding impressed as he sat down. "We have made a big deal in this place, no?"

"Yes, a very big change to this simple village."

Busy eating, the man asked, "Who owns this place?"

Slocum looked at Angela for the answer.

"They said a man named Crawford, but he is in Mexico City right now. Salazar simply took this place over."

"A good thing for him that he was gone, or he'd be dead too, huh?" Obregón dove into eating.

Slocum, amused by the man's hunger, agreed and winked at Angela. "Obregón, you weren't hungry, were you?"

The man paused. Then he looked at Slocum and Angela like he had just noticed them. "This is such good food, I don't want to miss a bite."

He went back to eating, and they laughed.

19

"Where will he hide?" Angela asked, sitting up in the great bed, holding the sheet up to cover her bare breasts as morning light slipped into the room from behind the drapes.

Busy dressing, Slocum pulled on his leather britches. "A good question. Salazar left the live oak, according to Cherrycow, who tracked him out of the grove. He had to have some help to do that. Cherrycow thinks I hit him. There were spots of blood, he said."

"I heard part of that conversation. I hope he is right. Maybe Salazar will crawl off and die."

"I doubt we have that good of luck. But anyway, I think he'll go back to his headquarters and raise another bunch of outlaws."

"Using his power over their minds, huh?"

"It has worked so far."

"You are right."

An hour later, he and his men held a parley squatted in the lacy shade of a large mesquite. Few of the Cockroach's men could have escaped their assault. Several were blown up in the jail explosion, many more killed in the efforts of Slocum's men and the villagers to pick them off separately, and the Cockroach's *segundo* was no longer breathing.

"Will he run to Mexico City?" Angela asked them.

"No, his power is over the people up here. He will try to kill us. We are the only threat to his reign over these people." Slocum regretted not managing to shoot him the night before. Salazar was worse than a plague on these mountain people—getting control of their minds, then making them do criminal things for him. Of course, the rape and pillage they'd done to this village probably didn't take much encouragement on Salazar's part—but he still led them.

"So?" Angela looked wistfully at him. "What is next?"

"Sierra Vista."

"Ah, *sí*."

Two days later when Slocum led his crew over the pass, the red tile roofs of the peaceful village gleamed beneath them in the bright mountain sunshine. The sight made him satisfied that at last they had arrived. Gathering cumulus clouds had begun to form, promising a shower or two, as regularly soaked the afternoons. Maybe a drencher, maybe only a sprinkle, rainstorms kissed the mountains somewhere every afternoon. From the looks of the thickening clouds, the rain would soon start.

They rode directly to the great casa outside of town that Salazar had occupied before, but found it empty. No one was there. An old wood seller on the road said everyone there had left several days before, and he lamented that there was no one there to buy cooking wood. It obviously must have hurt his economy.

"Is it safe to go to your amigo's place?" Angela asked.

Slocum nodded, and they rode on to Don Carlos's house. The clop of their horses' hooves on the stone street was noisy, and his friend was on a balcony when they rode into the courtyard.

"Good to see you, amigos," he said to them, smiling at their return.

Donna rushed from out front door to be hugged and swung around by Slocum.

"How are things? Are you married?" he whispered in her ear.

"Yes, yes."

He set her down with a wink. "Good for you."

"Thanks to you, my friend."

"Quit flirting with my wife," Don Carlos shouted, and everyone laughed.

"You should have married an ugly woman. How could I not flirt with such a lovely one?"

His crew laughed, and they dismounted too. Angela ran to hug Donna, who told Slocum to follow them inside. Then the two females left him. Chattering like magpies, they sauntered back inside, arms hooked together, deeply engaged in a conversation.

"Did you get him?" Don Carlos asked when he came downstairs.

"Not yet. We had a close encounter two days ago. We took out his gang down at Los Piñones. He is not at the casa outside town here."

Don Carlos nodded. "I caught a hint about him. They say he is at the Hernandez Ranch on the Río Verde."

"We can rest our horses and head there *mañana.*"

"Good. I have some excellent American whiskey."

"Sounds good," Slocum said and nodded to the men to take care of the horses. He followed after his friend.

"How are things at the mines?"

"No problems. You have La Cucaracha so involved in getting you that he has no time for robbery."

"I may have wounded him in our encounter two days ago. Cherrycow said there was blood on his trail."

"Shame you didn't kill him. The son of a bitch." Don Carlos poured some whiskey into two glasses, then handed one to Slocum. "Here's to his death."

"I have him on the run. We'll get him."

"Oh, *sí.* But it would have been nice if he was already

dead." They clinked glasses and took sips of the fine bourbon.

Slocum nodded his approval. "The rope is getting much shorter."

"I hope that people appreciate all you do for them."

"The ones that count do." Slocum nodded and took another sip of the good stuff.

20

Slocum woke early and, after voiding his bladder, dressed and went to the kitchen area. He found the crew busy preparing breakfast. Donna blinked at him and then drew her bathrobe tighter and more proper.

"You are up early," she said.

He took a freshly made sopaipilla and a small honey bowl from one of the saucy-eyed younger girls. *"Gracias."*

Then he turned to Donna. "I wouldn't want to miss a thing that goes on down here."

She hugged him and pressed her hip to his. "Well, we are always glad to see you."

"I thought that now you are his wife, you would sleep in, huh?" The sweetness of the bite of food flooded his mouth.

"Being married makes no difference. I have to be certain everything is just so or I am not happy. How is the man's wife you retrieved?"

"Recovering. This business he uses is hypo—"

"Hypnosis. I have read about it. Do you think this is how he manages these people who work for him?"

"What do you know about it? I only ever saw one doctor

use it. During the war he did it to help wounded men through surgery without ether, to dull the pain."

"Mind control is what they say it is, but no one seems to know much else."

"Salazar must have gone to Europe and studied it over there. He's from a rich family, so it would be no problem for him."

She nodded. "Now, if I could use it on these girls." They both laughed.

"You are leaving today?"

"Yes, in a little while. The ranch is a two day ride. So we can leave at a decent hour for that one."

"Aren't you afraid he'll ambush you?"

Slocum nodded. "But I have good scouts."

"You must, and God also watches over you." She gave him a kiss on his cheek, then went off to organize something the girls were doing.

He and his "good scouts" rode out around eight o'clock, with the sleepy-eyed Angela shaking her head aboard the dun horse. Yawning big, she rode in close to Slocum. "I am not a morning person, I have decided."

"Oh, just now. You've been doing good though."

She forced a smile. "With you, I have to be." Then she openly laughed at something else and shook her head to dismiss it.

He'd miss her when all this was over. But he soon needed to meet a man about taking his herd of steers to Kansas. Time to get things ready up there. Walter Kenny expected him. The days had flown fast with all this tramping up and down the mountains. He hoped to close this matter soon and be rid of this Cockroach once and for all.

Slocum made arrangements with a small rancher for them to camp on his land. Hardly more than a boy, the rancher said he ran some cattle in this high country and also caught and broke mustangs to survive. His pregnant young wife carried a baby that still suckled her. But they were happy, and knowing they were a small subsistence farm, he made sure his crew ate from his pack goods.

From the stacked hides, Slocum decided the ranch family lived on deer meat. His name was Laredo and his wife's was Pia. Pia and Angela talked together much of the time they were there. Slocum felt certain that she did not have many females come around—she about talked Angela's ear off.

Later when they were alone in the pines above the ranch house, Slocum and Angela whispered to each other in the bedroll.

"You know she was sold at twelve to a whorehouse?" Angela asked.

"Who did that?"

"Her father."

"Nice guy."

"He also sold her two older sisters earlier to that same man. She doesn't know what happened to them. Laredo was one of her first customers, and later he took her from that place and married her in a church. But she worries that they still look for her."

"Probably she should."

"There is no way you can make her safe?"

He chuckled. "No, I have no great powers."

She snuggled her body suggestively against him. "I simply wondered."

He agreed and kissed her. In another day he hoped to confront the one causing all the current grief in this land.

The following day, they reached the ranch in late afternoon and were close enough to see cooking smoke escaping the casa's chimney. In the corrals, a handful of horses stood hipshot. They had been ridden hard and had dried salt encrusted on them from their hard push up there.

In his telescope, Slocum counted a half dozen armed men moving about the place. Night would take care of those odds. Slocum and the others moved farther away from the casa. Finding a fresh spring and a small valley for the horses to graze in, they camped for the afternoon until after dark, when Slocum planned to raid the place.

Being familiar with the setup of the ranch down there from when they had rescued Martina would make it easier for him and his men to take the place. He simply wanted to get Salazar this time. He was deep in thought when Angela joined him, seated with his back to a large pine tree.

"Where will you go from here?"

"San Antonio. I promised a man I'd ramrod his trail herd to Kansas, and that's not far away."

"You won't need me along, huh?"

"Trail driving is a tough business. Very remote country. We don't see much civilization."

"When will you return to San Antonio after the drive?"

"Fall."

"Can I figure on having a damn good reunion with you then?"

"That's long drive and lots of rivers to cross."

"For you, hombre, I can wait." Hands behind her head, she smiled as if in anticipation of the reunion event.

"What can you do in San Antonio until then?"

"Whatever. I'll be waiting."

"I might—"

She put her finger on his lips. "I will be waiting."

He agreed.

After darkness, he and his crew descended on the ranch. He told Angela to wait a ways back from the ranch house in a grove of pines until things were clear. Squatted down, he whispered, "If anyone finds you or you get in a tight place, remember, clap your hands three times—it might stop them."

She frowned at him. "Why is that? You said before it might paralyze them?"

He looked off toward the lights in the house and the Chinese lanterns outside. "It has to do with how his spells work. Just use it if you need it."

"Clap my hands three times?"

"Yes."

"I will."

He patted her leg and set out. Six-gun in his fist, he scrambled from big tree to big tree, looking for any signs of the guards patrolling the main casa. His men were coming in from various sides, and his plan to take all of them was ambitious. Lightning speed might do it.

Shots sounded from the south, and the guards directed all their attention in that direction. Then a stick of blasting powder went off. Men were screaming and stumbling around outside the house by the time Slocum reached the edge of the building.

With his right arm in a sling, Salazar shouted orders from the house. Satisfied that no one was behind him, Slocum stepped in.

"Don't move a muscle."

"Ah, I recognize that voice. At last we meet again."

"Salazar, drop the derringer in your left palm or die." Slocum cocked his Colt's hammer back with a click, ready to gun him down. His poised finger was on the trigger—the derringer clunked onto the porch.

"Good. Now move out of here, slow-like."

In the darkness, Slocum's men walked in holding Winchesters ready at their hips. They began to disarm the other gunmen, shoving them down to sit on the ground.

"Well, well, I underestimated you again," Salazar said.

"You've simply run out of your nine lives." He shoved the man forward.

"How is my lover, Martina?"

"Much better, away from you." Slocum was not satisfied that they had the entire place under control.

"What a shame, she was such a fine nymphomaniac, I miss her badly."

"She damn sure doesn't miss you—"

"Gentlemen," Salazar said with a new look of evil on his face. "My men, the ones you did not get, now have you covered."

Slocum saw them step out of the shadows with rifles in their hands.

Salazar laughed aloud at the new situation. He whirled and pointed his finger at Slocum. "Who do I shoot first?"

Then someone clapped their hands three times, and the armed men went stiff.

"Get their guns," Slocum shouted and dove for the man nearest him. He wrestled the rifle from the outlaw's hands and then whirled around to face the raging Salazar.

"How did you learn that?" Salazar snarled as the pistoleros took charge from the dumbstruck guards.

"It worked. It worked," the excited Angela cried, coming into the flickering light of the lanterns.

Slocum walked over and thumped Salazar on the chest with his index finger. "From the woman you abused."

"You can't do anything to me. The law won't let you—"

Obregón stepped in and clutched Salazar's bad arm. "Listen, hombre, we ain't taking you to no fucking *federales* for them to turn you loose. You killed my compadres. You raped some of the finest women on this Earth. There ain't a prison good enough for a damn cockroach like you."

"What—what are you going to do?" Salazar's face paled.

"Hang you," Slocum said. "When it gets light enough. You also killed a great lady I knew and liked."

Salazar sneered at him. "That whore was only bait."

"Like Obregón said, you will be bait yourself for the vultures and buzzards in the morning."

"I have money. Lots of money. How much do you want?"

Both men shook their heads. Obregón spat on him.

"Keep your money. It will make the fires of hell even hotter." Obregón turned on his heel and walked away, making the others line up the bandits, hands tied behind their backs. They stood hangdog as the sun first peeped into the deep valley holding the ranch.

Twelve blindfolded bandits stood before the barn. Obregón had cut out two youths from the gang and forced them to watch as three men were stood up, and then fell to the ground, each one shot in the heart. This was done four times, and Obregón was only forced to dispatch one who had not instantly died from the rifle bullets. Then he ordered the two boys to carry the bodies over and dig a large common grave for all of them.

A rope was fashioned into a noose, a saddled horse of the outlaws' was brought forward and Salazar was placed upon his back, the noose secure around his neck.

"You have anything to say?" Slocum asked him.

"Yes. You are making the biggest mistake of your life hanging me. My father is a very rich man. He will hire killers to track down each of you here today and kill every one of you. You must think about this before you hang me."

Obregón swung a coiled *reata* at the horse's butt and shouted, "Enough of you!"

The horse sprang forward. The rope creaked under Salazar's weight, his neck popped and he swung there—dead.

Silence fell over the watching men.

Obregón said, "We have buried the rest. He is not worth burying."

Two weeks later, Slocum and Angela were in the square in San Antonio listening to the strum of two guitars. Seated at a table in the shade with them was a shorter man whose weathered face was the color of good saddle leather. They sipped on their drinks. The other man wore a brown suit and appeared to be in his early forties. Walter Kenny's blue eyes sparkled as he leaned back in his chair and considered Angela.

"What in the hell took you so damn long in Mexico?" he asked Slocum.

"A cockroach."

He nodded his head like he understood. "They're tough critters to get rid of sometimes. And you, miss—why are you hanging around with him?"

"Oh, I'm not half sure." Amused, she wrinkled her nose at him.

"Good, you looked like a woman with good sense. I know that song they're playing. Let's you and me dance."

"Certainly." She rose and started to dance away with a wicked wink for Slocum.

Slumped in his chair, Slocum simply smiled back and drew a deep breath as he watched them whirl across the smooth rock pavement. La Cucaracha was dead at last.

Epilogue

Slocum left the Farmers and Merchants National Bank brick building in Abilene, Kansas, and stepped into the brilliant late June sunshine on the Abilene boardwalk. Walter Kenny's proceeds of $143,000 from the 1,912 head of three-year-old steers was bound for San Antonio via Wells Fargo. Considering Kenny's expenses at under $20,000 for help, supplies, horses and wagons, including paying Slocum's bonus for getting that many steers there out of 2,000 head—Kenny had a comfortable fortune headed his way.

Slocum looked up and smiled at the woman seated on the surrey. Dressed in a fashionable driving dress and a large straw hat on her head, she looked at him with sparkling eyes as he climbed aboard next to her.

"Well, Mrs. Cruces, let's go see the world."

"I may miss having a horse between my legs all day long driving this rig." Then she handed him the reins to the spanking team of driving horses. "I'm ready to go anywhere, sir."

Slocum laughed and clucked to the horses. "I'd kinda wanted to go see Chicago."

"I thought we were headed back to San Antonio?"

"Anything suits me, Angela. Anywhere you want to go suits me."

She hugged his arm. But before she could speak, a cowboy on a bucking horse who was blasting his pistol into the air came charging down Main Street. Shouting and hollering, he was waking up any late morning sleepers and clearing the street.

"Let's go anywhere then," she said and moved her rump over against him. "Anywhere will do."

Watch for

SLOCUM AND THE BIG TIMBER BELLES

389th novel in the exciting SLOCUM series
from Jove

Coming in July!

41543

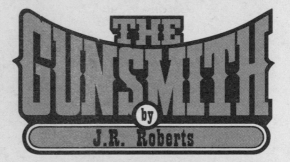